THE AMERICAS

Advisory Board

Irene Vilar, *series editor*

Also in the Americas series

A Stitch in Air

A Stitch in Air

a novel

Lori Marie Carlson

Texas Tech University Press

This is a work of fiction. All of the characters, organizations, and events portrayed in this novel are either products of the author's imagination or are used fictitiously.

This book is typeset in Minion Pro. The paper used in this book meets the minimum requirements of ANSI/NISO Z39.48-1992 (R1997). ∞

Designed by Kasey McBeath
Digital cover art created by Kasey McBeath

Library of Congress Control Number: 2013949635
ISBN (paper): 978-0-89672-813-4

13 14 15 16 17 18 19 20 21 / 9 8 7 6 5 4 3 2 1

Texas Tech University Press
Box 41037 | Lubbock, Texas 79409-1037 USA
800.832.4042 | ttup@ttu.edu | www.ttupress.org

To my beloved husband Oscar Hijuelos

Whose passing has rendered me to silence.

Contents

Two 1579

Three 1580

Four 1581

Lace is a thing sui generis, like nothing else made by man or woman. It is the response, the retort, the aesthetic contribution of our chattering, screaming, love-making, scrambling humanity.

John Cowper Powys

Fervent love can suffer much, tepidity very little.

Teresa de Avila

One
1578

1

reverie

Often as she went about her daily tasks, sometimes rushing to the hermitage to meditate or study her pattern book, Adela wondered why she had never been able to remember the face or figure of her mother. It grieved her. And, now, as she rested in the garden on a lovely afternoon, she was thinking yet again about that momentous day in 1566, the day when she, at five years of age, had entered the protective house of Saint Margaret in Granada. For upon that singular morn, when she had journeyed from her little village to the capital of the province, her world had changed for good.

The way by carriage had seemed endless; her mother more of an apparition than flesh and blood, and this is how she recalled her still: a shadow. On that ride there had been endless fields of barley and wheat along the country road, the fertile Andalusian meadows. And silence, except for the clip-clopping of horses' hooves, as they pushed farther and farther north under the fire of the sun. Suddenly, rising from the golden plain, she could see the city ramparts. As they reached a gate, the dusty road became a cobbled lane, and soon they were engulfed in a white-walled maze, wending round and round.

When the carriage came to a halt in front of an imposing arched door, her mother helped her down from her seat. They had arrived at their destination. Adela smelled the goodness of garlic toast and olive oil wafting in the air. "A monastery," said her mother, as she touched the girl's head tenderly. Yes, this she could remember: her mother's voice. And there little Adela stood, in her sack-frock and dusty leather sandals, waiting for the door to open. In an instant, with the creaky shutting of heavy wood, the city vanished with its noise and odors, business, and bustle.

Peace. The perfume of flowers. An immaculate courtyard, not a vagabond leaf in sight.

Within the confines of ancient Saint Margaret, only calm and beauty prevailed. The sound of water trickling from the fountain, the sweetness of orange blossom, the allure of jasmine and lemon. Everywhere she looked, she saw women dressed in white, gray, and black. The large lady who first took her hand smiled broadly in welcome.

"I am the abbess, sweet one," she had said.

Her mother vanished at that moment. Never to be seen again. But Milagros was there, too, standing quietly next to Reverend Mother and making quite an impression.

Milagros's eyebrows were straight and black, without an arch. And her eyes were warmth itself; a color akin to the darkest mulberry leaf or the richest earth. A dark green-brown. She was reed thin with sagging skin along her forearms. Her feet were narrow and long, fitted with black felt slippers.

Best of all, the kindly nun, sensing Adela's apprehension, had hugged her tightly in welcome. And then the two had walked to the kitchen to get some freshly baked bread and lemon jam. When Adela noticed the hot sun through the dirt-streaked windows, she asked, "May I have orange water, too?" for she was parched.

"Of course," Milagros answered. "But please, don't be so afraid of me. Why are you so afraid? I'm to be your *maestra*."

She had no answer.

And with that Milagros gave her a drink and, as a treat, withdrew some ginger sweets from one of the other sister's hidden stashes.

As Adela sat happily, enjoying those sticky nibbles, she made the acquaintance of the convent's cat, an old deaf calico. They played—

Adela dangling a string and the cat chasing after its tugs—and fast became friends. From that day onward, until the old calico passed away, she followed little Adela everywhere and at night took to sleeping at the foot of her bed.

Of course there was much that Milagros had to teach her charge, for under the abbess's instructions, the little girl was to be groomed as an artisan in the craft of lace, for which Saint Margaret was famous.

That very day, just after the noon-time prayers, after Adela had visited the statue of the Holy Mother in the chapel, Sister Milagros had taken her to the lace room, in the east wing of the convent on the first floor. It was a large, high-ceilinged space, different from the other monastic quarters; pristine in its cleanliness, it had many windows, which allowed the sun to aid the sisters in their exacting labors. The lace room's white walls bore the shine of alabaster. Bent over, in the throes of their intricate stitching, the sisters, young and old, were busily making their ornately florid tableaus—lengths of the finest cloth with depictions of every imagining: angels descending on earth, noble lords in their carriages, unicorns prancing in gardens, lions, and Christians in battle. But to the sisterhood of Saint Margaret, the lace room was much more than just a place in which such wonders were sewn. It was, as well, a chapel of womanhood, designed by the abbess to be such. The lace room was a reliquary of Saint Margaret's dreams and silent hopes.

There in that drafty space of calm industry, hung wispy lace ruffs, bridal veils, garters and chasubles, mantillas, delicate aprons, underskirts, cravats, handkerchiefs, bed sheets, and dresses in various stages of completion on cross poles, all waving softly under a breeze.

"Do you see, little one," began Milagros, as she pointed to a piece of lace fabric on her worktable, "this is *lacis*." And then she added, "How pretty is this little castle with the banner flying from the turret, no? And above you. Look at all the marvels. It is this handiwork that has conferred upon Saint Margaret the highest favor of the bishop."

Adela pointed at a veil and smiled. "Yes," she answered shyly.

"Our commissions throughout the kingdom, especially in Castilla, produce a handsome income for His Holiness," announced Milagros proudly. "And we receive commissions from Flanders and Sicily, as well. Why just yesterday Sister Inés began a trousseau for the Duchess of Parma. And tomorrow, María will start a bridal gown for our bishop's niece."

Finally Milagros directed Adela to a small table next to her own. Spread across the surface were strange and new objects to ponder: a large, sharply edged leaf, some pinkish shells, a tiny ivory dog figurine, a silver pomegranate, a painted black-and-gold fan. Adela meekly pointed to a red lacquered box. "And that?"

Opening up the little case, Milagros took out a pair of castanets. Holding them high, each in the palm of her hand, she began to play a frenetic clip. "When I am feeling tired, I make a little music, and then my work improves. But, now, let us concentrate."

Milagros sat down and spoke softly. "See, Adela? How carefully this must be done?" With a rapid and steady hand, the nun traced the leaf on parchment, using a small piece of chalk. Then, Sister Milagros encouraged the child to do the same. But as hard as Adela tried, she was distracted by what she saw through the window. Waving leaves in the air, silvery green. And then, a dove. Flying right then left, left then right, up to the sky. She couldn't help but run to the window, so mysterious was this activity. Her nose against the shutters, she finally saw the picture. Just outside, in the garden, two of the sisters, Isabela and Victoria, in their long beige habits and expansive wimples, were tossing an egg back and forth between them. But what were they playing? Adela put a cupped hand to her eyes to get a better look at the game. Ever so carefully the two nuns went on, stepping further back with each catch, and laughing, as if they were children. And just then, as they were standing some twenty feet apart, the egg burst open, yolk and transparent fluids, spreading like an opening blossom on the prettier nun's long apron. And then they laughed again.

2

sanctity

It had been the abbess's decision alone to put Adela under the watch and tutelage of old Milagros. Who better among them, reasoned the abbess, to instruct the child of a poor woman who did not wish to have her daughter chained to the order for life? Ah, Milagros. Unlike the other nuns, all of whom had entered their life of seclusion as children, Milagros, before submitting to the cloister, had experienced the secular realm with its multiple splendors and misfortunes. She was, as the abbess put it, "wisened to the world." But such were the circumstances of her entrance to the order, that they would forever be kept secret. The Reverend Mother was especially discrete.

Within a few months of her arrival, Adela began to show an aptitude for the making of fine needlework under Milagros's careful guidance. It wasn't easy at first. Mishaps and subsequent bouts of tears were common in the child's daily lessons. Once, she pierced her left little finger with a dramatic thrust of her right hand into the tissue of the linen backing. "I can't, Sister Milagros," she cried out. She jumped up and ran from her chair, the needle still in her pinky. "I will never learn," she yelled, as she raced down the hall.

Eventually, however, with her nimble, childish hands, she learned to stitch trim work with silk and linen thread for the delicate borders of a handkerchief or a chalice veil. Soon enough, she showed such a facility that it seemed as if she had been born for the task. Never complaining, and always eager to begin her work, each day found Adela in her little chair next to Milagros, watching and imitating her teacher.

And she got to know the others. On any morn that first year, Adela's eye would fall on another child of her own age, the little Isabela. Possessed of the straightest nose, dark blue eyes, as purple as the myrtle flowers on the garden path, she resembled a cherub in a chapel painting. Within her always shone a happy light, as if she were lightness itself. In the back of the room, near the door that led to the refectory hall, sat ancient Juana. Her wheezing coughs came and went to a rhythm as mysterious as the shadows passing over the large stone floor. They, in turn, prompted complaints from ill-tempered Clara, who was forever asking the offending sister to "please be quiet" and "tame the beast within." Sister Inés hovered over her cloth, as if inscribing stone, her spine a jagged curve, her unadorned head of long white hair bobbing up and down as she remembered a tune she had heard from the gypsies in her youth. A wicked tune at that! And María, whose digestive health was delicate, made hiccups that could cause the cat to whine endlessly and put everyone on edge. But, of them all, Adela remained particularly curious about Sister Dulzura, who sat beneath a large painting of the Virgin and Saint John the Baptist. From morning to afternoon, Dulzura threw sharp needles at the other sisters' heads for sport.

3

harmony

Those days passed in agitated defiance for some, simple resignation for others. For not a one, save for Inés and María, had willingly desired the cloistered life to which they were to be always bound. Their lives had been decided by imperious fathers, brothers, uncles, guardians, for the most part—on a whim, on a bet, on a drinking binge! Men who thought it paramount to protect the honor of the family by stowing away the "female element," that which could so easily bring shame on the family name either by indiscretion (oh the shame of a wanton girl! so weak, so light of mind) or the inability to marry well for lack of funds (the infernal cost of matrimony!). But the sisterhood, however upset or disappointed by their fate, did admit to loving their home, for the convent was well appointed, pleasing, and lovely in design. The most beautiful in the land, according to the abbess. And the sisterhood was given an unusual amount of freedom, for the abbess was a rebellious sort. A very independent thinker. Particularly when it came to the edicts of the bishop and his circle; commands designed and implemented by "those poor ridiculous impostors," as she was wont to say every now and again.

Their imperious commands and rules were always an attempt at stifling their spirits. And from whence did this contrariness spring forth? A keen observation, over many years, of the shenanigans of priests coupled with a feverish devotion to Mary, Mother of us all and guiding light in darkness and despair. And Mary's very own concurrence, spoken one night during Lent, "We must forgive the men in the world—and there are not a few—who bring about such pain in the lives of women. And we must, Abbess Ana allow our faith, as women, to be natural to our form. For we are healers. We live not for power but for love. And my hope for Saint Margaret is that there be kindness and harmony within her walls. Your devotion should be free of fear."

And it might be said that the abbess was also influenced by the advice and counsel of her beloved brother Don Ramón, who was most successful in affairs of business. Although he had found his fortune in the New World, in Lima, to be exact, he never failed to discuss the abbess's accounts and ministrations in the many letters that the two exchanged by way of galleon.

Adela and Milagros sang in harmony as they looped and pricked, carefully composing and building upon an old pattern for an alb, stole, or collar in *punto in aria,* or "stitch in air." This was a basic stitch, a small little loop sent back on itself, but one upon which all others depended. The loose, light netting was an exercise to promote steadiness of mind and hand. Each thread filament was as light and artful as a snowflake, for the threads that constituted lace were born of inspiration from above.

Whenever Milagros looked over at her pupil, she felt an abundant pride. Despite her youth, Adela had a rare intelligence and a kindly disposition, and, as an artisan, she had already evinced an intuitive eye for harmony and balance. She had even developed a stitch of her own, a small loose knot, irregularly shaped like a seed pearl. Milagros marveled over its intricacy.

"And how did you come by this?" Sister Milagros asked the child, one fine spring morning.

"By looking at the dress on Our Lady in the chapel," she had answered, with a catch in her voice, not looking up from the work in her hands.

"Well then, however you do it, keep on, and give thanks to *El Señor!*" Sister Milagros told her, in wonder over such a natural talent.

And Adela surely gave thanks after her day's tasks in her favorite place, the chapel. She loved it, for it was the Virgin Mother's sanctuary. Each time she visited the incense-laden room, with its pink marble altar, she sensed the Virgin Mother's soothing presence. Freshly cut jasmine adorned the altar. And tiny votive candles flickered in the shadows. To the left of the altar stood a large wooden statue of Christ and to the right was a life-size statue of the Holy Mother herself, Mother of the Rose, the exemplar of suffering, the source of all that was purity. "Remember, Adela," Milagros would often say to her pupil, "that we are reminded, as we work, of Mary's spinning skills, a sign of her perfection. As Saint Anthony of Padua has said, 'Out of the sackcloth of our nature Jesus Christ made a tunic for Himself, which He made with the needle of the subtle work of the Holy Spirit and the thread of the Blessed Virgin's faith.' And yes, too, we look to our Blessed Mother for the patience and grace to accept our lot in this life, however heavy."

Adela knew that the abbess felt a special bond with Our Lady the ever Virgin Mary. In truth, a most unique bond. There was gossip among the sisters that on occasion the Holy Mother conversed with the abbess, explaining her needs and wants. At Christmastide she hungered for red cherries, and at Easter, she requested strawberries and cream. One particularly damp and chilly January she even asked the abbess for a woolen shawl trimmed with silver lace for she "did shiver upon Twelfth Night."

And so Adela asked Milagros if such gossip were the truth. "Does the abbess really talk with Our Holy Mother?"

"Yes, my child," replied the kindly teacher, with a wink.

For all Adela's wanderings about the convent, she was most happy in Sister Milagros's company. Working side by side, they whispered the kyrie eleison, and this invariably led to an oft-repeated conversation.

"My dear child, do you miss your mother?" asked the teacher.

Silence.

"I believe she loved you dearly."

"Perhaps. Perhaps not. And, well, I hardly remember her now. Only her voice. High, yet soft, like that of the bird outside my window, *maestra*. But, truly, I'd rather not talk about my mother, if you please. For if I do, I will certainly cry."

Of course, as a dedicated convent artisan, Milagros's thoughts often turned to matters of faith. Intent upon giving Adela an education rich in Biblical literature, she patiently described church symbology. As for the latter, Adela knew that the lily and the pomegranate, the tree branch and the leaf, the lamb, the rose, and the carnation, and most importantly the Tree of Life were popular and lovely forms to sew upon the cloth. But the doting teacher had also instructed her pupil to study the abstract, geometrical attributes of lace work at its best. The Moorish motifs of Granada, in lovely star-like repetitions and ornate leaf, were not to be shunned but rather embraced even though they were most true to the Mohammedans. She explained that the reconquest had been achieved after long, bitter centuries of fighting. But the kingdom, however Catholic, owed much of its artistry to the Moors. "They were once preeminent in this land. Do remember that, my dear. The others here will not admit it. And I will tell you something more. Eh? A little secret just between the two of us. On each and every piece I sew, I leave a prayer to Allah."

There were lessons of life and ancestral legacies, also, which the sister wished to share with her pupil. Learned truths spun from the will of the Almighty and woven from the hardships of fate that must be told. These were the real treasures that Milagros had to offer her charge.

4

rosary

Long before she had decided upon the time and manner in which she would convey to Adela the gifts of her heart, she had committed them to memory. Like a rosary prayed silently. One by one, flower by flower, they rested in the place where knowledge and unknowing meet: in the mysterious folds of the soul. She hoped they would serve as the wellsprings from which Adela's imagination, tenderness, and artistry would grow.

Having loved the girl from the moment she was given watch of her, the elder vowed that Adela would have a rich, unlimited womanhood, not the life of a novice. In this, her way of thinking differed from the sisterhood. But Milagros's nature had been singular too.

She had known riches and love, a large and adoring family as a child, and happiness of the conjugal variety as a very young woman. Milagros had married a man of wealth, a trader of silk and elegant cloths whose many journeys across roiling seas took him to Tunis, Damascus, and Persia. And it was on the ocean that he had perished, in a storm.

A young widow, she had lived alone in the grand house that her adventurous husband had worked so hard to build in the Albaicín of Granada; he himself never had the pleasure of knowing that domain in its finished magnificence with its resplendent architecture and blue-and-white-tiled walls. Its completion came two months after his death.

Alone and bored in the budding years of womanhood, Milagros had turned to sewing, embroidery, and the craft her mother had taught her as a child, that of creating *lacis*. In the large house with its many rooms, nearly empty all, she would wander and think about the designs of fancy she would bring to life. Sometimes she would take a roll of precious velvet and make a dress or cape. Occasionally, she would embroider a bed cloth for a friend. But most often she would sit in the parlor on the first floor, near the interior courtyard, and create a piece of lace, delighting in the precision and concentration that such work required of her. It helped to quell her grief. And it was a welcome distraction when dark forces began to descend on her. A Morisco of uncertain allegiance to Catholicism, she was all too vulnerable to the passions of the time. Given the feverish pitch of the Church, the authorities had visited one too many times to ascertain her true devotion to "the one and only faith." And she had her suspicions that a servant in the household was acting as the Holy Office's spy.

5

legacy

Never having spoken of her worldly years to any of the sisters, save for the abbess, divine providence had finally granted Milagros the moment in which to pass on the memories and thoughts that she had guarded in silence for so long.

Taken by a chill one morning and retiring to her bed, the old woman knew that the angel of death was knocking at her door. There was something about the smell of the air, the cast of light upon that morning. Violet. And she heard the strains of a lute, a sweet, luring song that seemed to tell her that heaven was calling.

The end of her days was approaching, yes, and it was Adela, now seventeen, to whom she would unlock her heart.

She had pondered this special moment for months, as the abbess and sisterhood had fussed to heal her, as they labored over their syrups and potions and consulted countless medicinal manuals plucked from the convent's library shelves.

Lying in her little cot, Milagros eyed the goings-on about her with amusement. *Whoever would have thought my life would end like this*, she wondered to herself, *among a community of nettlesome Catholic nuns.* Life was, indeed, a mystery.

Since falling ill, her days had begun with the abbess knocking at her door to see if she felt better, and always Milagros would answer, "I am the same, dear Reverend Mother. Neither better nor worse." And then Isabela would enter with a bowl of broth, feeding Milagros as if she were a baby. "Now, open wide, *hermanita*," she would whisper. "There, there. Sip slowly." Isabela was so sweet, thought Milagros, as the young nun would wipe away the dribble from her mouth with a little cloth. And then Inés or Clara might follow with a censer of lavender and a special prayer mumbled in Latin.

There was the time when María had rubbed her neck and back in goose fat saying all the while, "This is what my mother often did to me when I was stricken with a fever. It will help, dear Sister." On another occasion, Dulzura almost succeeded in trying a more novel, therapeutic approach. She had entered Milagros's cell near midnight, invisible in the dark, saying, "It is I, Dulzura. I have come to take away the poison in your system. This will hurt, but you will be the better for it." Her intention had been to bleed Milagros with the sharpest needle she possessed. Most fortunately Adela, on her way upstairs, had heard the stirrings coming from her teacher's cell and intervened before Dulzura could attempt her foul deed.

Finally, the convent had sent word of the suffering ancient to the finest physician in Granada. After many attempts to vivify the ailing soul with infusions made of saffron, mustard, and oil of baby eel, he, too, reluctantly, admitted defeat.

Yes, thought Milagros, my time has come, as she struggled to breathe, feeling the tightness in her lungs.

But she had one last request to make of the abbess before leaving the temporal realm. Knowing that her hopes for Adela depended on the grace and understanding of the Holy Mother, she wished to ask for a special dispensation for her pupil: that, henceforth, the child be given the key to the convent to come and go as she pleased; a privilege heretofore of the abbess' alone.

When the abbess arrived that morning, she closed the door behind her and went to Milagros's side. She knelt down slowly and began to say the rosary. And then the two women prayed aloud:

Let nothing disturb thee,
Nothing afright thee;
All things are passing;
God never changeth.

Milagros softly stated her will at last, stopping every now and then to take a shallow breath. And the abbess, upon hearing the fervor of her entreaty and the clarity of her reasoning, agreed to everything she requested. After the two old friends recited a Paternoster, the abbess departed. The sisters, one by one, came to say their farewells. And, then, it was Adela's turn to say good-bye. She rushed to her beloved teacher and began to weep.

"My child, do not be sad," cautioned the dying woman, "for I go to a better place." Taking Adela's hand in her own, she whispered, "But first I must tell you of wondrous things."

6

solemnity

That afternoon a solemnity never before experienced by the sister-hood fell upon their house. Their cherished Milagros had passed from the earth. And the communal grief was great.

In response to their sadness, most of the sisters chose to abstain from the evening meal, preferring instead to fast as they prayed for the soul of their departed.

The abbess went to the chapel to kneel before the Virgin Mother. For three hours, she prayed for the safe journey of Milagros toward the celestial orbits of paradise.

Adela, who had gone to her room after her private farewell, wept until she fell asleep. And when, finally, she sat up on her cot and stared out at the starry sky, she came to a conclusion—only in cre-ating something from the depths of her being might she be able to truly honor her teacher and everything she had given her in life.

And, so, she began a pattern for an altar cloth on the very evening of Sister Milagros's passing. It was just after vespers.

Without making a sound, she passed through the house's wind-ing halls and hurried to the lace room. Not a soul, except for a field mouse. She could hear the creature scurrying along the floor.

The abbess had forbidden the nuns to work in the evenings, as such hours were dedicated to prayer and meditation only. And she would not have her children work by candlelight, for the Holy Mother had said to her time again, "Be gentle with your flock, dear Abbess. Rest should come with evening." This once, however, Adela could not obey. She felt the urgency of putting down on paper her inspiration; otherwise she felt certain she would forget the ornate design.

She tiptoed to her velvet cushioned chair.

Taking parchment and a piece of chalk, she quickly sketched her plan: a pomegranate—the symbol of Granada—in the center, flanked by interlacing stars and bordered by roses. In one corner, the lower left, a small branch of an olive tree, a tiny dove upon it: her signature.

That night the lemons of the cloister garden were ripening and the scent was heavy in the air. Through the open windows the citrus permeated the room, entering Adela's breath and pores. A perfume as powerful as an opiate. Yet on she worked with the help of the obliging moon.

In silence and in contemplation, the intricate design progressed. Her teacher had parted from the earth, it was true. But her lingering spirit provoked such tenderness that Adela was surprised by the intensity of it. She felt Milagros's presence everywhere, as though her soul were the very air itself, boundless and infinite. And while she worked, she pondered the whims of her own existence. For though she never spoke of the questions and circumstances of her birth and subsequent life in the convent, her doubts had kept her shy and unsure. Who was she really? And why did her mother leave her with a house of nuns? Who was her father? Why could she not remember anything about him?

Perhaps, she thought, it might be possible to find peace in the freedom afforded her now: in the dowry of secrets revealed by her teacher upon her last hour.

She worked as never before, with a passion for living, in adoration of nature, in reverence of the extraordinary woman who had been like a mother to her. And, yet, she felt lonelier than ever.

"The lace maker must be humble in her enterprise," she had been taught. Was it humble to attempt so magnificent a cloth? And yet she was making a covering for the altar in remembrance of Milagros and the *reconquista*. Should not such a mantle be inspiring?

She sought to understand humility. Was it denial of self? A discipline of the heart? Lack of pride? Obeying the will of God no matter the consequence? She wanted to be excellent at her craft but she most desired to be modest. She wished to achieve, yet she hoped to be a servant to others.

She reached beneath her collar and touched the hidden necklet from which hung a tiny glass ball. Inside, a yellow fleck; one of Sister Milagros's parting gifts.

"Any time that courage fails you, remember the mustard seed," she had whispered.

In another ecclesiastical residence that night, a servant was handing an epistle to the prelate of Granada. After heaving his girth upon an ornate setee, the bishop opened the letter to see that it was written in the hand of his beloved sister, recently widowed. She was asking that he make provisions for her in his fair and noble city, among a community of goodly nuns that "she might meditate and find the word of God" to comfort and guide her "in the ways of Our Lord." She felt "guilt extreme." Her poor husband's death, she noted, her fault. "I fed him far too many *morcillas*, marzipans, and ginger creams. The physician told me that his bloated body was directly a result of a diet too rich for his system. How can I ever be forgiven, dear brother?"

7

sanctuary

The bishop, having meditated on his sister's needs, concluded that the Convent of Saint Agnes would be an ideal sanctuary for her. The Convent of Saint Agnes was a small, congenial, and temperate monastery, just outside the city gates. A simple house devoted to prayer. In humdrum constancy his sister would mend, he felt certain.

High-strung and of a spirited temperament, Soledad Paz had been of a fragile constitution since babyhood. A quiet, highly ordered abbey was what she needed most at this difficult time of mourning. Yes. Saint Agnes, he thought.

But, then again, might not Saint Margaret be a more judicious choice? The food produced in that lovely domicile was the finest of any he had tasted in the land. And if his sister were to be a guest there, he might find occasion to visit more frequently. The partridge, the very rare chocolate. The saffron buns. Oh, just thinking about such luscious foodstuffs made his stomach grumble. Saint Margaret, then. Yes. Saint Margaret.

He quickly penned two letters of instruction: one to Abbess Ana and the other to Soledad Paz.

8

clarity

The day following Sister Milagros's death, a thunderous storm erupt-ed. Rain fell from the heavens with cooling clarity, lifting away the pollen of the Andalusian fields for miles around. Kneeling in prayer, in a dreamy state, at first Adela didn't hear the sound of laughter coming from the garden. But after a crack of thunder, echoing three times in the distance, she heard a young nun shriek. Adela stood up and looked out of the window toward the orange orchard. A figure dressed in gray was running through the downpour, giggling as she ran for cover. Her face turned up, her mouth wide open, the playful nun was gulping the rain. Then, she began to dance the saraband, her arms above her head. Isabela.

Remembering Sister Milagros's feeble voice as she struggled to impart the first of her secrets, Adela crossed herself. "On a night when the moon is round as a melon, go to the old Moorish palace. It is a place abandoned and neglected now, but all the same, a worthy destination. I've heard that the King and Queen occasionally visit . . . to remember the origins, the old customs of our people." This the old woman had said with a small squeeze of Adela's hand. "Perhaps you will go only once; or perhaps you will go often. Either way, may the first vision you have last all the days of your life. Carefully observe the handiwork, the composition of the interior. It is lace of stone most rare. Lace of stucco and marble. The palace shows us that starlight can be captured by mortal hands. Adela, make your lace . . . like starlight."

When Adela had heard these words, she wondered how it could be possible to make cloth glow and shimmer. For starlight was such an elusive gift. By what combination of elements might this be achieved?

As if decreed by Milagros's spirit, a full moon presented itself that night. Adela watched as the soft turquoise blue of the sky turned black as ink, and there, above her head, a pumpkin globe appeared. It hovered gently over the earth.

The moment had come for adventure, an escapade foretold and encouraged by her beloved teacher.

Excited, she threw on her cloak, carefully covering her head and face. Then, ever so quietly on tiptoe, she left her cell and rushed to the convent garden, letting herself out through the locked gate. As she quickened her pace on the road before her, she wondered if a vigilant sister might have heard the unfastening of the rusty latch. And if so, what envy and gossip would prevail. But soon her attention was elsewhere. She marveled at the beauty of the streets. She was free and this was a glorious night, indeed. She had not anticipated such loveliness awaiting on the other side. Looking about, she admired the cascading red and pink geraniums upon the walls of the city. These blossoms filled the air with spicy sweetness. Peering up toward the sky, she saw the great hill where the palace was to be found. And then, as she rounded an alley, she saw the edifice itself. Under the light of the moon, the Alhambra sparkled like sunstone for its facade was a honeyed red.

As she neared the rolling gardens that surrounded the complex, she stopped abruptly. Orange groves flanked the path. Before her were blue roses. She stopped to pluck a bud and breathe in its subtle perfume.

She sat down on the ground and thought about the hands that had built such a dwelling. The men who had raised its ramparts, tiled its floors. She imagined its past inhabitants, the men and women who had walked its halls, dreamt by its fountains. Were the spirits of those occupants still present in the sound of the wind, the scent of the flowers?

But enough of her musing; she had work to do. She must find the elusive caterpillars who would be her helpmates. She knew the creatures were to be found in the ancient mulberry trees that were planted by Granada's merchants long before she was born. "Just beyond the principal gate, which is called the Gate of Justice, among the roses," Sister Milagros had advised. "There you will find them."

With basket in hand, Adela walked toward a spot thick with vegetation and knelt down. Sure enough, she saw a carpet of gold, rippling like water. The caterpillars were abundant. But they seemed to appear and disappear in the blink of an eye. Deftly she scooped up the creatures—two, sometimes three at a time—in the palm of her hand. Gently, she laid them on a bed of basil in her basket. When she felt certain the number was adequate to her task, she left.

Back at the convent—out of breath, for she had run all the way—Adela went to her garden hermitage. When she opened the basket to peer at her catch, she whispered, "Now begins our work, known only to the saints and the seraphim."

9

gaiety

The abbess woke up suddenly, tugging at the edge of her cot. It was not yet morn. Was the strange tale she had dreamt a premonition or a very clear message from Mother Mary herself? Perhaps it was a warning of laxity and excess or the dire consequences of not following the rule. Then again it could be a figment of her worries yesterday, following a visit from the bishop. He was adamant about his sister staying at Saint Margaret, and he repeatedly emphasized that she be treated with all good grace. Before taking his leave, he said, "I know that she will appreciate particular attention to her diet. She is a woman of ascetic taste."

Sitting up, now, the abbess slowly rolled her body sidewise to set her feet down on the floor. Yes, yes every detail was so clear as if she had lived it. First, she remembered walking through the courtyard from her private quarters toward the main house. She heard the campanile's morning song—jubilantly rhapsodic, as if declaiming a holy feast day. When she passed the rectangular garden at the edge of the courtyard, she abruptly stopped. The geese and mottled hens were strutting about within the monastery compound where they were strictly forbidden. Proceeding down the path, she shooed away the honkers and rubbed her eyes. Did her vision fool? For next to the gurgling fountain in the center stood a tree of exuberant color. Just looking at this fanciful tree made her feel joy. Stepping closer she saw that this wonderful thing was a folly of marzipan adorned with little fruits in the same. (Ah, thank the Moors for that confection!) Tiny purple grapes, pink peaches, yellow apples, plums. She snatched a few, made the sign of the cross, and put them in her buck-toothed mouth. They were *divinos*.

Upon entering the main house, she turned right and hobbled down the hall to the refectory door. Steadying herself with a treasured cane (all silver-made and worked in flowers), she peered inside the spartan room of dark beamed ceiling and simple white stone. Great garlands of flowers, green and crimson, fell from the oil lamps lining the walls. Pink petals carpeted the hexagonally laid, red-tiled floor.

The long oak table was covered in pearly satin, one of the better cloths in the house. Upon it was a royal feast. Not at all a poor Lenten meal of fish broth and bread, befitting a time of fasting and self-restraint. No, not at all. This was an abundant repast of delicacies. She spied pigeon pie, suckling pig, and saffron cake in syrup. Sherbets of lemon and orange rested on ice blocks. Fluffy scrambled eggs with nubs of bacon and yellow onion beckoned. Mounds of chicken rice. Flaky pastries stuffed with peach and quince. And there was a keg of bubbly wine.

The sisters were stuffing their mouths with golden, fried sparrow wings and succulent honey figs. Moaning in a completely inappropriate manner. And, oh dear Victoria, the most circumspect among them, was smacking her lips and sucking noisily on a knuckle of pork fat. The abbess winced upon seeing threads of lard dripping down Victoria's whiskered chin.

That morning, the convent's meditative order disappeared. A celebratory air of gaiety and chaos was everywhere. Belches and burps flew in all directions. Isabela, clearly tipsy, was dancing to the squeaks of the *gaita*. Who would have thought that partridge-faced María, of the wobbling bottom, was a natural at blowing on the old goat's bladder! Inés was singing at the top of her lungs.

But as the abbess surveyed this scene, she noticed that Adela was not among them. Perhaps, she thought, the pretty young girl was still in the kitchen laboring over her cauldrons and ovens.

The abbess then passed through the refectory, turned left, and entered the kitchen. Not a soul to be found.

Painstakingly she made her way upstairs to Adela's room at the end of the dormitory hall. She knocked four times and then called out, "Child, are you there?"

And then the dream had slipped away.

She patted her pillow and lay down again. Closing her eyes, she made the sign of the cross. Should she understand this as a warning from the Holy Mother? Something was awry, some air, some strange inhabitant of thought, and she must set the convent right before a soul or two were lost among them. Yes, this she must do. A pilgrimage?

10
liberty

Adela worked best on the altar cloth in the early hours of the day, when light bid darkness farewell and took her sovereign place. Adela's golden caterpillars also did their finest work at dawn.

Careful to follow the instructions of Milagros, she had done exactly as the old nun had advised. For weeks, she had given the insects their daily nourishment of rice paste, freshly made each day, so as to make the creatures healthy. The recipe was simple. First, she cooked the rice in a fowl broth. When the rice was boiled well, she poured it into a large wooden bowl, adding salt and a cup of olive oil. With a strong wooden paddle, she crushed and stirred the ingredients until a smooth, silky mixture was formed. On this food the caterpillars had grown quite large, too large to be kept in their basket. Their new home was an abandoned hutch, carefully hidden within the hermitage, a little wooden hut that had been used by Milagros for private meditation.

Whenever she had found a moment of liberty, she went to the orchard to find the stones that were to serve as "the canvas" upon which the design of the caterpillar lace would take shape. As the stones were too heavy to carry, she wheeled them by cart to the garden hut. And as soon as she had gathered together ten that were adequate in size, she began the process by which she would work. For caterpillar lace, Milagros had said, "was made in quickened time, according to a predetermined measure."

"Take the paste and spread it over one stone. Make certain that the paste is layered evenly and of the thickness of your small finger," she had instructed. "Next, and this is important, Adela," she had whispered with a nod of her head, "you must draw your pattern on the surface quickly. Use a good olive oil, a young green oil as your ink. A fine brush. Draw your pattern well. And when you are satisfied that your design is near perfect, only then, take the stone and stand it upright against the wall. Finally, place the caterpillars on the earth at the base. They will recognize their food. Then their work begins."

And it was so. Quite so. For in the weeks she had been preparing her stones, one by one, she had learned just how clever a lace maker the Alhambra caterpillar was.

Each and every time without fail, their lace work was beautiful and of a delicacy and strength unequaled. As the furry golden creatures crawled up the stone to consume the paste, they made a web-like net of silk. Never touching the lines of repellent oil, their design took shape against the pattern reversed.

As stone upon stone yielded to lace, Adela carefully brought each piece of cloth to her cell. She stacked them one upon the other, underneath a sheet.

She did not derive pleasure from secrecy, but she wished to keep the work from view for she knew the others would note its rareness, and then, there would be questions. In what way was such a lace achieved? She had not thought to ask Sister Milagros about the manner in which she should answer.

One morning after she had tended to her lace work and her chores and made the sisterhood a hearty breakfast, Adela heard four knocks upon the door of her cell.

"Adela, it is I," said the Reverend Mother, "come to talk to you about a serious matter."

As the abbess labored to enter Adela's room, the unmistakable scent of carnations filled the air. (It was said that the Holy Mother bathed in water with these flowers, which she grew and tended solely for this purpose.) A large and fleshy woman, she possessed a constitution that was temperamental at best. Since her childhood, she had born the cross of cricks and cracks. Her spine, her hips, her knees and ankles swelled whenever it rained. Or whenever she was particularly agitated (the nasty Dulzura provoked this tendency). And when such occasions were upon her, she suffered in silence as she struggled to keep her stature upright and correct. Such was the case on this morn.

"This compartment suits you well. The light is good. And the view is inspiring, I think," she said as she stood swaying in front of the window.

"Yes, Reverend Mother."

"I have come to speak to you of something that relates to the sisterhood."

"Yes, Mother?"

The abbess sat down on a small cedar bench, and Adela, likewise, sat on the edge of her bed.

"Child, I am making a pilgrimage to Santiago. I shall be away at least six months. And I would like you to preside at Saint Margaret in my absence. You have a good head for housekeeping and a sensible way with the others."

Taking in this news, Adela closed her eyes. She simply could not imagine being the abbess's substitute.

"But Reverend Mother," she stammered, "Sister Clara, perhaps, would be a more commanding presence. She is very organized. And rather bossy, too. She is far better suited to governing than I. And what of Victoria? She is capable. And wise. And just imagine how Dulzura will react to my being her superior. You know that she has never liked me. Even as a child. Why I remember her putting beetles in my soup."

"Because, quite simply, choosing among them will stir their rather contentious natures. Don't you think? Heaven knows there is enough jealousy and bickering already in this house. And never mind Dulzura. There are malevolent spirits within her, as very well we know. She was born of a wicked womb. May Jesus Christ protect us from her." The abbess crossed herself. Then, looking at Adela with a smile, she said, "I have decided that you are well disposed for this. The matter, as I see it, is settled."

Adela, rubbing her hands, tried yet again to persuade the abbess otherwise. "But," she started again, "what of my work? I have just begun a special piece, the labor of which is dear to me. I will not have time to pursue it."

"I will ask Sister Isabela to assist you. She is capable, you will see. All will be fine." And with that, the abbess concluded her remarks. She got up slowly, rubbing her left hip.

Then, just as she was about to leave, she hesitated.

"There is one thing more, my dear. There will be a guest at the abbey in my absence. The bishop's sister is coming to spend a few days in meditation. She will reside in my quarters. I understand that she will be accompanied by her spaniels. I am certain all will be fine. Just use common sense. Well, then, I will see you at supper this evening."

Adela resumed her meditations, considering the situation before her. It was true that the sisterhood was prone to gossip and quarreling; no doubt the fact that she had been chosen to govern would not be taken especially well, either. She was among the youngest after all. But she was afforded a certain respect by most, as she had always tried to comfort and help her sisters. It was her "maternal nature," as Isabela would say. Far more worrisome was news of the bishop's sister, which likely meant more visits by His Holiness, too. This, in turn, would mean greater household care for everyone (the bishop was a demanding man, often requesting a change of bedding twice daily, flasks of wine on the even hours, and a thorough dusting of his rooms in the morning and the evening); better, more costly food, for the bishop's palate was exigent; and, most regrettably, renewed tensions among the sisters, allowing for tiresome complaints about slights, mishaps, and annoyances.

11

finery

Shortly after the abbess's ceremonial departure from the convent—
there had been a special mass offered up for her protection on the
camino delivered by the prelate himself—the bishop's sister, Soledad
Paz, came calling. And sure enough, she was accompanied by ten
excitable spaniels, her beloved companions. The entourage's arrival
was announced by the reverberating howls and ceaseless scratching
of the animals' paws upon the great oak door.

"What is that racket?" growled Sister Clara, as she limped down
the staircase from the second floor. "Ah, yes, the bishop's sister. A
slothful soul wanting to be treated like a princess in our midst. Well
I, for one, will not have it. No." At that moment, Sister Clara's only
audience was the child Beatriz, who, upon seeing the ill-tempered
nun, put her fingers in her ears. Not even the adorable little Beatriz,
recently arrived at the convent, had patience for the mumblings of
Clara.

Adela, followed by Isabela, quickly went to the great hall. Together they opened the massive door. No sooner had they done so, the
sisters were met with a waft of rancid air. The tawny-fleshed spaniels,

it appeared, had not been bathed in quite some time. In the background, Clara shrieked, "And they stink of rotten curd, as well, these intruders."

"I am fatigued," announced Soledad Paz, as she stood before the opened door. She was a tall, imposing woman who bore the haughty air of a duchess.

After two attempts to pass through the opening, she complained, "What a meager entrance, dear sisters." So wide was her skirt and so broad her veil that she could only enter the portal sidewise.

"The journey was so very tiring. Tiresome in the extreme. And my dogs are excitable. The problem of being in such a miserly coach all this way. Would you have any suitable food for my sweets? They are fond of calf livers."

Adela introduced the bishop's sister to Isabela, saying, "Isabela is assisting me in all household matters, my dear lady. Anything you have need of she can provide, I am certain. And, now, please follow me as I would like to show you to your rooms."

"Very good," answered Soledad Paz, managing a tiny smile. But she feigned approval. Such a young, witless girl in charge of the order? With dogs in tow, she followed Adela to the rear of the convent garden.

Upon entering the abbess's quite luxurious quarters, she looked around her carefully. The abbess, while sometimes lax in following the rule and rather scatter-minded in her approach to household management and business, did have an appetite for fineries. Red brocade, ornately patterned and thick as leather, enormous swaths of it, draped the windows of her apartment. Tooled silver boxes, small and large, decorated her tables. Little ceramic bulls stood here and there. And plush divans and chairs in deep green satin added regal elegance to her domain.

Such riches in a place of prayer and meditation? Did they not honor the vow of poverty? Furnishings of this luxury were not to be found in her own home, not even in her brother the bishop's palace.

She sat down and began to wriggle her feet; then she cleared her throat and, raising her legs a bit, shot Adela with a disgruntled expression, saying, "Have you no manners? Now pull off my boots, would you?"

And when Adela had obeyed, removing Soledad's hand-sewn kid boots, Soledad held her arms out wide so that the poor girl might attend to her clothes, which, though drowned in perfume, and despite her aristocratic standing, were rather rank. Aware of a prickly rash blossoming on her chest, the widow took a black silk fan from her purse and said, "I think that we shall stay a month. I am seeking God's mercy, and I must find penance here." Then, she began to weep softly, adding, "My husband's untimely death is my fault, you see. All my fault."

Adela tried to be attentive to her guest's laments, but as much as she tried to comfort her visitor, she was preoccupied. She had much to do. Too much to do to prepare the sisterhood for the evening meal. The bishop had informed her that he would be dining with them that evening. From previous visits Adela knew that the bishop was particular about the order and quality of his meals. Broths and small dishes of carefully seasoned vegetables were offered first to whet his appetite. Roasts, joints, and platters of rice were to follow. Sweetmeats and pastries at the end.

When Adela had finally finished putting Soledad Paz's garments away in a chest, she bid farewell, saying, "And now my lady you must rest. Dinner is at 6:30."

"Will silence be observed during meals," asked the still sobbing widow. "For I wish that it be so."

Attempting a courteous response, Adela replied, "Normally, we do not adhere to rules of silence during meals. We are rather informal here at Saint Margaret. But I will see to the matter. And, now, I will leave you to your rest. Isabela will come in an hour to attend to your needs."

"Yes, well I need a chamber pot most urgently," answered Soledad Paz.

Adela closed the door thinking she should never have agreed to the abbess's plans. She should have protested strongly. Running the convent was too great a burden. And she was worried. Silence had not been observed during meals for years, not since the abbess had decided that conversation during supper would benefit the spirit of their community. She tried to remember the signals used for such an occasion. She had forgotten them, save a few. Scratching one's nose meant *I would like another helping,* curling one's tiny finger meant *please pass the wine. Another helping of meat* was making a fist. And *rice please* was rubbing both hands together.

To help her prepare the others, she went to the library and quickly composed a lexicon. This she would ask Isabela to distribute at once.

12
sobriety

That afternoon, Adela, with the help of three trusted sisters, rushed to the henhouse for eggs, teated the cows for milk puddings, pulled radishes and lettuces, and ground spice for stewed fruit. She was making a special sweet, a saffron cake with pomegranate sauce that made the bishop swoon, as if intoxicated. (Once the abbess had confided to Adela an indiscretion. His Holiness upon eating three helpings of this cake was so giddy—no one knew he had poured an entire bottle of brandy on that dessert before devouring it—that he took a ride down the banister of the stairs and landed with a frightful thud on his back.)

When the bishop arrived by carriage that evening, Adela greeted him with a curtsy and kissed the large ruby ring on his right hand. His scent of lavender water was nearly overwhelming. And she noted, too, that in one month he had grown thicker, much thicker, in the middle. His large gold cross jumped against his waist with every step he took.

As she led His Holiness through the door and down the corridor to the refectory, she felt slightly nervous. But upon seeing his enthusiastic reaction, his clapping of hands, at the richly prepared table, the rhythm of her heart began to settle. The long plank table was covered with a satin cloth upon which the house's Dutch china, silver utensils, and Venetian glass goblets were set. The silver candelabra, ten in total, bore sandalwood wax.

The bell tolled six o'clock. At that precise moment, the sisters with Soledad Paz and her spaniels left the chapel to make their way to the refectory, all the while singing with feigned reverence *Te Deum Laudamus.*

When everyone had gathered round the table, each behind her chair, the bishop and his sister took their places of honor. The spaniels lay down behind their mistress. Finally, Adela made a signal to be seated.

Isabela entered the room with an enormous platter of roast chicken and duck. Nearly tripping on the hem of her dress, she bowed and curtsied, offering drumsticks and breasts, wings and thighs, with a flourish of poetry. "A breast as tender as your bishop's," she whispered to the prelate with a wink. "And for you, Señora Paz, a cherub's wing. Delicate, sweet."

After the honored guests were served their generous portions, the sisters took their meager share. But then Sister Clara, without any warning whatsoever, interrupted the solemnity of the meal by standing up and sticking her fingers in her nostrils while pointing to the dogs. Juana did the same, although trembling. Adela knew without doubt that the signal meant *please more incense.* And so she rose from her chair and quickly went to the cupboard to retrieve cloves and dried roses. Filling the fumigation vase above the table, she caught sight, out of the corner of her eye, of one insolent dog relieving herself in the corner of the room and quickly doubled the amount, spilling the flowers and spices on Soledad Paz's head in the process.

Soledad Paz bristled at this carelessness. What an incompetent. And how dare she be treated so.

Returning to her seat Adela noticed that Juana was tapping her mouth with her thumbs. Was it pepper she wanted? Adela couldn't recall, but she passed the pepper all the same. But Juana shook her head and tapped her mouth again.

Adela looked around the table and saw that Victoria was furiously rubbing her cheeks. And at that very moment Isabela walked into the refectory with two more heaping dishes. She proudly displayed before the bishop a platter of crispy pork in one hand and in the other a compote of stewed oranges and onion.

His Holiness, intently eating from his heaping plate of succulent fowl and golden rice, seemed not to notice all the quirks and gesticulations going on around him, but Soledad Paz watched carefully. Her cheeks were red. Her eyes were burning black as she followed the sisters' ticks of the eyes, noses, and eyebrows interspersed with scratching, sneezing, coughing. Why they were making a mockery of her, were they not? Getting angrier by the minute with such foolery, she bit her tongue to keep from crying out her disapproval. Finally, she clapped her hands to stop. But clapping hands had a meaning, too: a command to generously burp. A *thank you* to the cook. And most unfortunately, Juana, frail as she was, had a monumental burping capacity. Her sign of gratitude rang forth with sonorous ease, provoking guffaws and giggles from the youngest among them, little Beatriz.

13

litany

The dinner came to an end but the evening was far from over. The bishop, in accordance with ecclesiastical law, now went to the library for an audience with each and every nun who had a grievance. Depending on the month or year, such an evening could last beyond midnight or it might be a merciful one hour. On this occasion, the sisterhood was in an agitated mood. Each nun, except for the child Beatriz, Adela, and Isabela, walked to the hallway to stand in line awaiting her turn to speak of her misery.

Sitting in a grand oak chair, its velvet cushions piled high, the bishop took in the opulent surroundings of the reading room. Saint Margaret's had, indeed, become quite impressive. He admired the beautiful paintings of Saint John the Baptist, Saint Agnes, and Saint Michael framed in heavy gold leaf work. Along the south wall, facing the orchards, he noted several large pictures of unusual charm: archangels with arquebuses in various poses. Some were defiant and others triumphant. And the tapestries on either side of the door were of feathers, bright yellow and blue. Yes, the convent was a wealthy one, wealthy enough to purchase such remarkable embellishments and portraits. Were they too wealthy? Were they keeping monies that rightfully should go to the Church?

Sighing, he reached into his pocket and took out a little bell.

With a flick of his wrist, the first confessor appeared at the threshold and closed the library door behind her. Kneeling before His Holiness, she began her litany of woe. "I must tell you of our mother's neglect," began María, the stoutest sister at Saint Margaret. "Your Holiness must note my swollen condition. It is owing to the quality of our wine, Your Grace. It is foul. And thick with sediment. Truly, it is thick as cream. And wine as thick as cream is inexcusable, as I am sure you must agree, for the hard-working sisters of Saint Margaret. We make a handsome income for the Church, do we not?"

The bishop closed his eyes and, putting his hand on María's head, responded, "Yes, yes, now. I will see to the matter. You may go, my child."

Next was Clara. Round of shoulder, heavy of step, she scowled as she approached her confessor. Around her neck hung several heads of pungent garlic. No delicate nun was she, thought the bishop, not even as a novitiate, when she might have had the blush of youth. "Please come forward," he said.

Clara stood erect and stern. "I have come to speak of the quality of our food," she began. "While His Holiness, this evening, was treated to an exceptional repast of taste and delicacy, you must be made to understand that this is rare at Saint Margaret. Our food, most often, features salted fish, gristly pork, and disgusting terrines of heaven knows what. My liver hurts each day, Your Excellency. My belly is emboldened. It rumbles and squeaks. Why the child Beatriz will not come near me. She pinches at her nose; she puts her fingers in her ears whenever I pass by. I beg of thee to talk to Sister Isabela of this matter. She is a frightful cook. Most terrible. I am an old woman. And I know you agree that I deserve decency, respect." And as if to emphasize this point, she jabbed at the air with her fists.

"I have made note of this," the bishop responded, wearily. "And now you may leave, Sister."

As Clara made her way to the door, she turned abruptly and repeated, "Salt cod, hocks, and tongue terrines. Imagine!"

The bishop removed a white silk handkerchief from his robe and wiped at his brow. But yet again he rang his bell for the next nun in line.

In walked Dolores, an amiable and even-tempered soul. "My only concern, Your Holiness," she began, as she curtsied ever so shyly, "is that our mother, our dear Mother Ana, will be gone such a long time. I miss her very much. More than you can imagine. Could you pray to the saints for her speedy return?"

Such a sweet request by such a kindly nun was followed, nonetheless, by the accusatory wailing of Dulzura. And Dulzura was a name as mismatched to her person (for sweetness she was not) as the peculiar tinted eyes, one soot, one saffron, in her head.

"Now what," muttered the bishop under his breath. Sister Dulzura had been a vexation to His Holiness and everyone else for that matter at Saint Margaret from the moment she had entered the order as a maiden and taken her vows. Even the abbess crossed herself whenever she saw Dulzura. Some of the sisters, Adela among them, thought of this virago as a cross to bear, a test of forbearance and patience sent by the Lord. But there were others who believed quite differently and thought she was, simply, the fruit of Lucifer. The bishop had his own view. He equated her with a bit of muck.

"Your Grace," she garbled. The bishop cringed at the assault to his ears. "I have come to tell you that there are heretics in our midst. Surely by now you must know that the young girl Adela plays games with Lucifer. I have seen her in the garden at midnight. She works her magic in the hermitage; of this I am sure. And the sister Isabela is her acolyte. She too plays with Beelzebub."

"And just what are these two girls doing that is so ghastly bad?" he asked with annoyance. "Would you tell me?"

"Well," the nun whispered, confidingly, "I've seen the young girl Adela doing strange things with stones that she gathers from the field. And she makes noisome potions in the kitchen."

"Stop," the bishop ordered, raising his index finger. "I have a question for you, Sister Dulzura. How is it that you know of this? What are you doing in these hours of the night? Should you not be asleep or in meditation with Our Lord? Go now and be done with you."

But the shrewish nun continued, nonetheless, waving a nasty finger in the air. "Mark my word, Your Holiness. They will bring shame upon us all at Saint Margaret. And maybe upon you, as well. The Inquisitors will surely hear of this sacrilege. And all of us will end up on the rack!"

Finally, yanking at Dulzura's sleeve, he pushed her out the door.

The bishop looked before him to see that a dozen nuns were waiting patiently for their turn. Putting his head down, he quickly walked to the kitchen and asked that Isabela, who was washing dishes, provide him with a flask of strong wine.

As soon as she decanted the intoxicant, the bishop lifted the flask to his mouth and gulped heartily. Fortified, and in a slightly better mood, he wobbled back to the confessional room. Could it be true, he wondered, that the young women were guilty of such serious charges? The pretty Adela and the equally fair Isabela? He wondered if this was mendacity on the part of the old crow or if there was something to it.

Later, that night, after he had finished his duties, he went to speak to Soledad Paz.

"One of the sisters has made claims against the postulants Adela and Isabela. I don't know what to believe, dear sister. Have you any thoughts?"

"Brother, yes; those two are frivolous in the extreme. And the luxury of this house. What is one to think of so much grandeur in a nunnery?"

"Hmm," responded the bishop.

"Brother, are you hearing me?"

"Yes, yes, dear sister. Well, then," he responded as he patted his sister's hand, "watch them carefully. Be my eyes and ears."

The following morning, Adela met with His Grace in the chapel. The bishop presented her with a list of improvements he felt prudent to pursue. Amongst the most urgent was the necessity of good wine, for after he had swilled the contents of the flask he had been given the previous evening, he had developed a mind-numbing headache and dragon stomach. Sister María's description of its quality was all too correct: thick with resin and suspicious of taste.

"The sisters might get poisoned from this dubious source of fortification," he advised. "I have heard rumors that some vintners in the region have been adding cow's blood to their product. Or perhaps someone here has tampered with the wine? What is your opinion?"

"I can assure you, dear Bishop, that no one at Saint Margaret's is fooling with our wine."

"And how do you know this?" The bishop squinted his eyes.

"Because Isabela and I take care of the pantry and the kitchen, Your Holiness."

"Well, then, you must talk to the merchant who sells you this wine. See to it."

"Yes, of course, Your Grace," answered Adela as she led the bishop out the door, confused by his brusqueness.

14

mercy

Life at Saint Margaret's had become more difficult, indeed, thought Adela, as she busied herself in the garden and tended to her herbs and lettuces. The reverberations of the disastrous dinner had made the bishop's sister a nuisance to them all. The convent had become even more of a squabbling hen house with Soledad Paz in the mix.

The bishop's sister, to Adela's dismay, had begun to study the sisterhood each morning in the refectory, sitting back in her chair and glaring at the women as they supped. Taking only a cup of broth herself, she clearly showed her disapproval of the others' hearty appetites. And more than once she slapped the hand of little Beatriz. "Don't you know, child, that one should eat sparingly? One roll is enough. No more, for you," she would say again and again, causing Beatriz to cry. During the mornings and the afternoons, she spied on the sisters as they worked and worshipped. Often she would stand in a corner of the cloister or blend in the shadows of the chapel during prayer time. Sometimes she would enter the lace room, circling around with a suspicious air. And she seemed to pay too much attention to the work of Adela. It was not uncommon for Soledad Paz to stand directly behind her as she worked, which made Adela nervous. More worrisome still; Adela had seen her approaching the hermitage at dusk, cupping her hand to her ear as she leant against its door.

Under surveillance, the bickering among the sisterhood had reached a climax. They were crankier than ever. Squabbles erupted over the smallest of grievances. Even the spaniel pets of Soledad Paz were an issue. Their stench was nauseating. And the one time that Clara had tried to wash them resulted in mayhem. The lye soap she used was so strong that their coats had shed, leaving sores on their hides. The dogs had yelped in pain without stop, and Soledad Paz went into a rage, screaming so loud that the sisters feared she had truly lost her wits.

Adela spent most of her time attending to these endless arguments and concatenations. Even Isabela, such a mild-tempered woman, was at odds with several of the older sisters who complained about the richness of the kitchen's cookery.

"Sister Adela, I must speak to you about an urgent matter," said Isabela one morning, as Adela kneaded bread dough. "Sister Clara is giving me headaches over her complaints."

"And what are the complaints?"

"She says our recipes are too spicy and rich for her constitution, that we use too much pepper and fat in the stews, and that we need to prepare food of a blander flavor. She suggests we eat porridge for our morning meal."

"Well, dear, why not prepare blancmange for her and let the others eat meat and preserves?"

"I offered to do that. But she complains that the vapors of the bacon are enough to sicken her."

"Isabela, do not worry. I will speak to her. Perhaps she will consent to eating alone in her room."

Such were the problems she experienced in her role as the Reverend Mother's minder. Most troubling was the little time she could spend in the hermitage. She meant to check on the caterpillar work, but it was impossible. The few instances she had managed were interrupted by the spaniels that followed at her heels and barked to high heaven. And even though the abbess had assured her that Isabela would assist in the daily administrations of the convent, Adela had quickly discovered that Isabela's nature, while straightforward and congenial, was not designed for such a purpose. Hers was a playful and free-spirited disposition.

Furthermore, Adela's frustration with the progress of her altar cloth had rankled more than usual. She had stayed up for weeks to work on a section that had perplexed her, as its execution was more difficult than any other stitching she had attempted.

Exhausted and bewildered by her inability to solve the problem of combining the reticella stitch with that of Gros Rose, she had fallen into bed without as much as taking off her slippers or her day dress one particularly hopeless night, falling into a deep sleep. Yet hearing shrieking, crying, and the clattering of pots against stone, she awoke with a start.

15

charity

At first, she thought she was having a nightmare. She had heard so
many tales of horror from Dulzura, of late. Talk of the Holy Office,
gruesome accounts of the Inquisitors' work to rid the land of heretics
and unbelievers, misfits, and miscreants. Jew and Moor. "They use
the rack," she taunted gleefully. "They pull them apart, bone by bone,
as they scream for mercy. They burn evil children and men at the
stake and hang old witches to cleanse the kingdom of putrification."

Adela's stomach would turn upon hearing of such horror. And
she would weep, albeit privately in her room, after hearing these
tales. Yet, again, she could not understand the ways of the world.
For didn't God's love show mercy, compassion? Sister Milagros had
taught her so. And Sister Milagros had confessed something else on
her deathbed: That the abbess had received her into Saint Margaret
when she, on the run from those very same Inquisitors, had barely
escaped death. "I ran to the convent, having heard of its charity, and
our mother opened the door and took me in. And it was by virtue of
our abbess that I found the essence of love. Acceptance, compassion.
Forgiveness. Our Holy Mother embraced me as if I were her own,
never minding my inheritance," she had said.

But, there, another high-pitched wail and a deeper bellowing. Adela sat upright in her cot to better listen. Then, there was a pounding on her door. She opened it to find a tearful Isabela.

"What is it, dear?" asked Adela, seeing the frightened nun in her nightdress.

"A bull, Sister Adela. A bull is on the loose. And it is in the convent, heading toward the lace room. Victoria has gone to little Beatriz. What should we do?"

Adela grabbed her shawl and took Isabela by the arm. "Come, come, let us go down the back staircase."

As they rushed down the second-story corridor, they heard a concert of howls and moans. Then, just as they reached the broad stone stairs, Adela caught sight of the bull's back end, turning a corner toward Sister Clara's room. A crashing boom ensued, followed by the soaring screams of the ill-tempered nun. A kind of sobbing echoed throughout the convent. "San Antooooooooooonio."

Having reached the first floor of the house, Adela and Isabela stood as if transfixed by the trinity, as the bull, with Sister Clara hanging on to its back for dear life, came racing toward them.

"Run, Sister, run," shouted Adela to Isabela. And run they did, past the lace room, the library, refectory, and kitchen. They ran as never before through the darkened Saint Margaret, and into the moonlit garden. Turning to see if the bull was on the chase, they fell into each other and landed on the ground.

The bull indeed had followed their course, and zigzagging round the columned portico, it crashed into the walls and terracotta urns of flowers, upsetting the meticulous work of pruning and planting.

Finally, after circling twice more, the angry beast attempted one triumphal leap, throwing Sister Clara free. Then, veering left, the indefatigable bull shot through the broken gate and out into the fields beyond.

Sister Clara lay at the base of the fountain, sniveling and gurgling. Not quite dead.

That night Soledad Paz shouted at the top of her lungs that she was "through with such a wretched place!"

She would report to her brother, the bishop. She would tell him all she knew. He would know how to deal with such wicked creatures.

16
delivery

No one, least of all Adela, expected the abbess's return on the Feast of the Assumption, for the Reverend Mother's pilgrimage was intended to be arduous, done in utmost reverence and penance; a long journey by mule coach and on foot. And Santiago was a great distance from Granada.

It was August; only two months had passed since the abbess's departure.

The sisterhood, except for poor, battered Clara who was recovering from her ordeal, had been singing the Angelus in the chapel when the unthinkable had occurred. Surrounded by great garlands of pink roses hanging from the ceiling all around, the sisters were trying to sing as sweetly as the scent in their midst. "*Angelus Domini nuntiavit Mariae,*" they intoned, some high and crooning, others hoarse and unsure. The chapel door opened and shut with a reverberating bang.

"My dear children, I am back," announced the abbess, as she struggled to stay upright. Hardly a sister among them recognized their Holy Mother. She stood trembling in her shredded cloak. What a phantom sight. She was thin as a wick. Her hair was a nest, entangled with hay, dust, and insects.

Using a staff for support, the abbess hobbled toward the sisters. She waved a bony hand in the air as she continued, "I return to you not nearly as well as I used to be, but nonetheless whole." Adela, seeing that the Reverend Mother was about to collapse, shrieked, "*Aguardiente*, Isabela! Go to the kitchen. Fetch *aguardiente*."

As Isabela ran in obedience, several of the sisters lifted the abbess from the floor and carried her to the infirmary. Immediately noted was the lightness of her body, as if she were a ghostly figment rather than flesh and blood. The Reverend Mother's face was drawn and colorless.

Gently she was placed on a cot.

"Is she alive?" asked Clara, who, nearly crippled though she was, had ventured out of her room upon hearing the commotion. Adela took a cloth and dipped it into the urn of holy water. Dabbing it on the abbess's forehead and cheeks, she answered, "She is breathing, yes."

In the days that followed, the abbess was revived with the hearty mutton broths of Saint Margaret's kitchen and the stimulant of brandy wine. Ever so slowly, she began to recover.

In the second week of her convalescence, she was taken to her own comfortable quarters. Amidst the familiarity of her belongings and the administrations of her children, she began to get stronger. Her renewed and more sanguine state was revealed in the blush of her cheeks, her laughter, and a desire to tell the story of her journey. (It must be said that the sisters had been anxious from the start to know what had befallen their beloved abbess, but none had the courage to ask, so respectful were they of her privacy.)

On a blustery September Sunday, just after lunch, she called the sisters to her apartment so that she might share with them the sad and terrifying details of her pilgrimage, cut short, before she had reached the place where Saint James's body lay, the Cathedral of Compostela, or "field of stars."

As the sisters gathered round her bed, she began. "I hardly know what to tell first; so many incidents conspired to detain me from my purpose. Although I suppose I might begin, my dear daughters, with the toad."

"The toad?" asked Adela.

"I'm afraid so. A most peculiar large toad."

And then small Beatriz asked, "What color was the toad, Mother?"

"It was purple. The color of a bruise upon one's flesh. With horns of red."

There was total silence in the abbess's room. Some nuns crossed themselves, others began to whisper the rosary under their breaths, but all were fixed upon the figure of the woman who was about to begin her tale.

"Well, I had been on the pilgrimage road for days and had reached the outskirts of Córdoba. It had been raining hard. So hard that the carriage in which I was traveling was suddenly engulfed by a river. A river where no river had run before; such was the force of that storm. And then before my eyes I saw that wicked toad jump from the current through the carriage window. It landed on my lap."

"What did you do, Reverend Mother?" asked Isabela.

"Well I tried to use my staff to toss it out, but that creature was too slippery and fast for me. It jumped from place to place, landing on my feet, my head. It made the most awful croaking. I was shrieking, too. Finally, as the carriage washed upon a bank, the carriage driver heard the commotion and came to my rescue. He was able to remove the varmint but only after quite a struggle, and I had made my escape."

The abbess sighed. "Well, after that nothing was quite the same, as before. We did arrive in Córdoba that night. But the inn was full except for one small room near the kitchen. It was frightful, my dear children. Wet and cold. The mattress upon which I lay was infested with vermin. And the air reeked of old goat cheese."

She looked around her at the sisters, one by one, all of whom expressed their horror with little cries of "Oh, Reverend Mother, no" and "poor Mother."

"I developed an all-consuming fever. And with only a thin cloth to cover me, I was shaking uncontrollably. I began to think that the Lord Our Savior was testing my resolve and faith, for surely I did suffer. So I determined to accept my sorrows with forbearance and began to thank God for allowing me such small grievances as compared to those that Christ endured for us upon the cross. I thanked Him for these tests of faith. For you see, my daughters, I undertook this pilgrimage at the urging of our dear Mother Mary, that we might bear witness to the glory of Our Lord and Savior. We must be prepared to serve God in our weakness and in our strength. And we must be on alert for the temptations of the flesh."

"What happened next, Mother?" asked little Beatriz, as she curled a lock of hair around her finger.

"The following morning, upon waking from a fitful sleep, I took some breakfast. A small cup of broth and a bit of bread. When I went to find the carriage, a stable boy explained that my driver had left the inn. Apparently our carriage had sustained damage from our journey. One of the wheels was broken. And he . . ."

Just then the abbess fell silent. The sisterhood, thinking that her exhausted condition was the cause, patiently waited to hear the end of her sentence. Smiling in an encouraging way and staring at their beloved prioress, they failed to see what was happening in their midst. A miracle of sorts, or if not a miracle, a sign of holiness. The Reverend Mother was stunned not by fatigue nor the infirmities of her body nor the painful recollections of her journey. No, no. The reason for her sudden loss of speech was the child Beatriz. Not quite five feet, but four feet at least, was her body above the floor.

"Beatriz, our dear little Beatriz, has found favor with God. Look!" said the abbess in a near whisper. "A levitation."

And indeed it was so.

A collective *ahhhh* filled the room.

And little Beatriz? Giggling beyond delight. For if she forced herself to touch the floor with her feet, she immediately bounced up in the air and proceeded to lie stretched out, first on her stomach, next on her back, now waving her arms, next wiggling her toes.

"Can you make yourself come down?" asked Clara.

"Yes and no," she answered. "For I do not know how this has happened. Something within me, like a little bird, has taken flight. I want to come down and be among you, but a hand keeps pulling me up." Then, looking at the abbess with the widest eyes, the child asked, "Reverend Mother, is this the hand of God?"

Willing herself to return to terra firma, she finally did. But Beatriz's status among Saint Margaret's sisters had changed in seconds from "the child" to "the favored one."

And then as if nothing remarkable had just happened, the abbess continued on with her story. "Now, where was I?" she asked smiling, as she beckoned Beatriz to her side. "Ah, yes. The carriage driver. Well, he never did come back, you see. And there I remained. Alone, quite sick, and without any means to proceed. I decided to spend another day at the inn to regain my strength."

"What happened to the driver, Mother?" asked Isabela, as she tenderly patted Beatriz's head.

"I will never know, but I must say that I thought from the start that he was rather strange. There was something about his character that did not seem trustworthy. Well, the following day the stable boy was able to replace the broken wheel. And I decided to carry on alone."

"But Reverend Mother, you have never driven a carriage. How is that possible?" asked Adela.

"My dear daughter," the abbess replied as she closed her eyes, "faith. It was faith that sustained me. And I knew the Lord was by my side." And then she slowly blinked while looking up at the ceiling. "I was, after much effort and hardship, able to journey farther north to Mérida. And this is where, truly, the devil sought to hold me back. For it was in Mérida that I faced the worst of my upsets. Oh, dear daughters, the thought of what happened in Mérida still pains me." Now, the abbess wept softly.

"What happened?" cried out Clara, as she fidgeted with her wimple.

The abbess cleared her throat. "What happened is I met up with bandits. The most awful of men. And they stole my mule and carriage. But then in the midst of my despair, I was visited by an angel of Our Lord, dear sisters. The angel pointed to a large almond tree whose shade was sweet. I sat down beneath its branches. And in my weariness and grief I fell into a dream. Our Mother Mary appeared to me and said that I should come directly back to you, my daughters, for there is a malevolent spirit threatening us, and we must gird ourselves against that which would harm, either common man or incubus. And sure enough, dear sisters, when I awoke there was a pilgrim bending down before me who said, 'Come with me. I will take you to a hospital nearby and there you will find succor.'"

While, with time, the abbess's health gradually improved, it was still uncertain that she would be able to resume all of the activities she once enjoyed, particularly her gardening. The abbess's arthritic hips had pained her from an early age, but her spirit of perseverance had served her indomitable will over the years. Although a poor administrator, the Reverend Mother's conduct as spiritual leader had been exemplary. And she would continue to act as the convent's spiritual counselor; on this point she was firm. Yes, having battled all manner of hardship—whether evil toad or flood or illness—the abbess was content to let Adela manage the abbey. She could see that the young woman had been more than capable in her absence. In truth, the convent seemed a more efficient place under her direction.

Adela, with an outlook as good as possible, carried on with her daily duties. Certainly, her visits to the hermitage had been shortened. She was sure to make the porridge for her secret caterpillar helpers, but no longer did she have the time to dillydally. In and out, that was the extent to which she stayed to watch them work on stone. And her own needlework progressed in fits and starts; a true vexation, as she had entered that stage of her craft when the excitement and thrill of seeing her vision take form had begun. This stage, set off by a kind of epiphany, had occurred without warning, as she was saying her prayers one evening. Something so simple, and yet profound, had happened. She had looked out of her window and seen a pattern of light in the sky. Not starlight, exactly. Something different. She wasn't sure what. But the elemental craft of luminescence against black had bedazzled her. And she thought that, yes, the making of lace could be like this, a kind of call in the wilderness, a cloud on stone, hope against despair and unknowing. Lace was like this, all of this. Something from nothing. And if she could, with all of her anxieties and insecurities, appreciate such subtle beauty in the firmament, perhaps she could learn to find a pattern like lace within herself. A different person within her person. Light. Texture. Love. Perhaps she was finding herself in the very altar cloth her hand had wrought.

In the end, whatever her misgivings, the abbess, knowing that she had burdened Adela more than she ought, assured her daughter again and again that she was free to do as she pleased, whether that meant working in the lace room after vespers or missing lauds and matins. She had, after all, made a solemn promise to Sister Milagros on this account and another, too; that she would not advise the young Adela to take her vows unless she herself desired it with all her heart.

17
duty

The bishop finished the last sentence of his report for the Holy Office with the sentence, "In all good conscience and with sole dedication to God the Father, I now await the directives of your graces on the matter of the Convent of Saint Margaret." Attached to his letter of condemnation was a list of charges made by Soledad Paz against the sisterhood with particular attention given to Adela's acts of magic and heretical depravity.

The bishop stood up from his desk and poured a glass of sherry. As he sipped his drink and devoured a handful of almonds, he wondered what might become of them, these sisters who had provided for the Church so handsomely with such exquisite laces. Why, in heaven's name, would they dabble in affairs of Beelzebub? Why would they bring ruin upon their persons and their lovely convent? And the matter of the bull with Sister Clara. Maybe their perversion was of a deeper, darker order than he imagined. An unnatural lust running through their veins. It was a confusing mess, for sure. But act he must according to his faith and in keeping with his highest calling, that of making sure his flock—nuns and monks alike—stay on the straight and narrow so that they might have eternal life. This was his duty. This was his sacred vow. He only wished that Soledad Paz had not been involved in this matter. How would it look to the Inquisitors? Had he not praised this community of sisters time and time again for their dedication to God and their commendable handicrafts? He would not be made the fool. He must by all costs prevent his good name from being soiled by this duplicitous nunnery!

18

curiosity

At first, no one heard the clamor of her fists against the hardwood of the massive doors. The bells were ringing to remind the sisterhood of their evening prayers. But after the last reverberation of a solitary chime, little Beatriz tugged at Isabela's sleeve and said, "There is a visitor. Listen!"

Opening the door with not a small amount of caution, for Isabela had heard from the bishop that there were thieves and ruffians about, she saw a woman before her.

"My name is Pilar. And I beg of you, Sister, to please give me refuge. For I am in need of protection." The figure at the door was bent to the ground, only her face turned up as she added in nearly a whisper, "This very night my husband searches for me to do me harm."

Isabela, without further thought, grabbed the arm of the mendicant and drew her within.

After Pilar had been given entrance to Saint Margaret, Isabela, followed by little Beatriz, led the woman to the cell that had been occupied by Sister Milagros. But not before taking a long look at the poor soul in need.

Pilar was the most beautiful woman that Isabela could ever imagine. Granted, she had not seen so many women, only those of the sisterhood and her mother. And, perhaps, her godmother? She wasn't certain. But this woman before her looked like the Virgin herself. Only fairer. Or so that is what Isabela believed. Her hair was the color of the sun, her skin as white as the moon. And her eyes so brown, so very dark, that her pupils were barely perceptible.

After filling the lamps in the room with oil, and lighting each one, Isabela finally showed Pilar to the baths and bid her guest goodnight.

Directly, then, after putting Beatriz to bed, she went to the abbess's apartment and knocked on the door.

"Who is there?" the abbess answered.

"Mother, it is I, Isabela. Come to tell you that we have a pilgrim within."

The abbess, slowly standing up, went to the door, whereupon the young nun told her everything she knew of Pilar.

The next morning, early, the abbess carrying a tray, upon which was arranged a meal of two rolls, a small flask of wine, some cheese, and sausage, went to the visitor.

She knocked four times and, while waiting for a reply, said a prayer for the soul on the other side.

Within seconds, Pilar appeared at the door, still in her nightdress.

"Welcome to Saint Margaret," said the abbess with a smile. "I have brought you provisions, some bread and wine. You must be hungry."

"Thank you most kindly, Mother," answered Pilar.

Immediately the abbess noted the refinement of her speech and glancing at the gown, which was draped across a bench, the grandeur of the bodice and skirt. Amethysts and pearls were sewn upon the silk.

"While you are here you may walk in the garden and the orchards. You may read in the library. Lunch is served at 1:00 p.m. and dinner at 6:30 p.m. We will have time to get acquainted, later. For now, I shall leave you to your privacy."

"I cannot begin to express my gratitude for your graciousness, Mother."

"No need, child. Rest now."

And without saying another word, the abbess hurried on to the chapel.

Although she had declined to eat communally, preferring to sip a bowl of broth or nibble at an omelet in the privacy of her room, everyone was curious about Pilar, who was most often seen strolling about the orchards in the morning, sometimes picking fruit. In the afternoons, she sat in the garden with a book in hand.

It was Adela who first sought out Pilar's companionship, thinking that the solitary lady might need a confidante. And she imagined that Pilar might feel quite lonely. And so it was that the two began an on-going conversation. And as it happened, Pilar was loquacious indeed. It seemed that, finally, after enduring ten years of the marquis's mischief in silence, she had taken a lover of her own, a young count whose virility was spectacular, a just rebuke for her roguish spouse.

One afternoon, Pilar determined to solicit the opinions of the nuns in her midst. What advice would they give to a woman in her predicament she asked of the small group gardening around her.

"I adore Don Antonio." Pilar clasped her jeweled fingers. "You see, Sisters, after many years of being neglected by my husband, the Marquis of Naranjo, after years of scant conjugal relations, let me emphasize, I have found a man who literally fills me with ardor. I hunger for everything about him, especially his thighs and stomach. Ah, what a stomach my Antonio possesses. He has a hair-lined chest that makes me swoon. As soon as he removes his shirt, I find myself aflame. And I cannot stop doing what it is I love to do. Once he overwhelms me with his *verso* and his *besos*, I am pudding. Complete pudding."

Isabela who was listening to each and every word felt her ears and cheeks burning to a crisp.

Adela, suddenly embarrassed, felt her lower parts tingle.

Inés, in the twilight of her years, thought back to the time when she, as a young novitiate, felt a sudden rush of excitement every time a certain bishop, Enrique, came to Saint Margaret to hold confessions. She thought Bishop Enrique had a handsome brow. And she liked his eyes. Kind eyes. Yes, she could imagine such a feeling of *pudding,* for her heart was reduced to such a mush upon those long ago visits.

"How did you meet Don Antonio?" asked Dulzura, as she probed her left ear with a twig.

"It was at a party. A marvelous party in Madrid, at the palace of the Duquesa de Liria, a most extraordinary woman. Do you know of her?"

The sisters shook their heads.

"Well, not important." Pilar stood up and pulled a lemon from a tree. Then, squeezing the fruit in her hand, she said, "This is the scent of the duquesa. Fresh lemon. With a hint of ambergris."

"I was sitting in the courtyard, as it was a terribly hot night. June. And I was fanning myself, when I saw the count come toward me. He was wearing black. A black silk doublet, a ruff of exquisite Venetian lace and a medallion on his cap of emeralds and gold. Oh, Sisters, he was a sight of magnificence."

Dulzura began to rub her backside.

Isabela felt the inside of her mouth begin to water.

And Adela? She thought of this count's kisses hot and rough against her lips.

"He said two words to me, Sisters. Two. *Mi vida*."

"And, what did you say, dear lady?" asked Isabela, as she put her hand upon her breast, for she felt her heart beat uncontrollably.

"Yours. Sisters, passion, the kind of which I share with Don Antonio is a powerful thing. I cannot forsake him. His sex is of a monstrous nature. And I am delirious when he takes me."

"How does he take you?" asked Clara, who was feeling a bit woozy, looser of stomach than usual.

"Like a bull, Sister." And she winked. "He takes me with one thrust. One long, very hard thrust."

In that instant, Isabela fainted.

After the sisters had revived the sensitive Isabela with a bit of shaking and cold water, directly on the face, Pilar decided it would be more prudent to discuss these tales of amorous intimacy in her room for any of the nuns who desired such an education.

In quick order, Pilar had assembled, in secrecy and discretion, a circle of sisters who wished to be tutored in the amorous arts. This was done by a nod of the head in the hallway. A smile. A touch of the ear, as if to say, "Yes, thank you, my lady. I will be present this evening. Grateful for your instruction."

Truth be told, the sisters had an urge so insistent for the details of carnal love that not even a worldly woman, such as Pilar, could have been prepared for the exacting questions she would be asked, almost nightly (after vespers).

One evening, a particularly curious group gathered around the beguiling adulteress, who now wore the old clothes of Milagros, washed and mended to the voluptuous measure of her figure. Pilar was sprawled upon the cot, fanning herself with a gold silk *abanico*.

"My lady," asked Sister María, as she wiped her brow, "can you tell us what the love of a man is like?" And this was followed by the stifled giggles of the others, as they bowed their heads and crossed themselves.

"The love of a man is simple, Sister. Think of a hummingbird. Does the hummingbird not dip into a blossom of crimson flesh, without a care? It is so with a man. He enters, with the right of a king, and stirs inside until the flower he has entered comes apart. The woman's petals, then, after a sweet agony, fall in tears and screams."

Adela followed with another thought. "Well, does this humming-bird not sing, as well? Or cry or scream?"

"Ah, Sister. This is a matter of taste. For some suitors make their ardor known like a violin, and others are silent as stone. It depends on the stringing of their vocals."

"How does a woman feel when she is broken like a flower?" asked Victoria, who was blushing to her toes.

"It is a state of such exquisite joy that words cannot describe. But let me try, however feeble my attempt."

Pilar, her cheeks ablush, closed her eyes and began to murmur. "First, and remember this, a woman is reluctant, ever so slightly, to let the hummingbird enter her rose. But, oh, sisters, once his needle pierces through the satin of her flower, she is his to feast upon. And he is hungry. So hungry that at times the woman cannot catch her breath. I, myself, have found that this state can be frightful. But there is always, always, relief, as if in a rainfall. The delight of the fall, sisters, is something that I cannot put to poetry."

"What is the fall?" asked Adela, who was secretly hoping to experience this ecstasy herself.

"Sister, the fall is the beginning of rebirth. Do you understand?"
Adela nodded shyly.

"After the act of love, a woman is as the purest babe again. She is destroyed and remade in one instant. And, my dears, this is why I cannot return to my husband. For Don Antonio owns me, every inch of my flesh, now. Please pray for me."

But for all of Adela's good intentions to keep the wayward Pilar in her prayers, she left with one thing on her mind alone: experiencing the passion of love herself. She remembered a scene she had witnessed the year before. There had been a wedding in the convent, a hasty wedding, on the eve of Good Friday. The abbess had arranged for the bishop to officiate—fortunately for the bridal pair, the prelate had stopped there to rest—and all had been arranged quietly among the sisters. The sisterhood had even managed to decorate the chapel with garlands of myrtle and jasmine in a matter of an hour.

The bridal couple was very young, the daughter and son of merchant families, according to the abbess. They had decided to marry against their parents' wishes, and the abbess had agreed to help them.

After vows had been taken and the sisterhood had bid them goodnight, Adela had decided to bathe. Walking toward the baths, she had seen the two young lovers standing in the courtyard, wrapped around each other. That look of pure joy on their faces, a kind of rapture, she had never forgotten. The image of them kissing had come to haunt her at the strangest of times, while praying in the chapel or washing her tunics or threading a needle. She could never predict when that singular moment—a young couple kissing—would play on her memory and cause her to wonder at the freedom of it. The tenderness of being in love.

Yet while Pilar might have need of Saint Margaret's and the sisterhood of Pilar, her visit was not destined to be long lived. For within weeks of her arrival, after a few of the older sisters—Inés and Juana particularly—began to complain to the abbess about a wave of inexplicable moans in the night, filtering through the walls and windows of the convent, the abbess decided to have a talk with their guest. And shortly, thereafter, the lovely *marquesa* decided to take refuge elsewhere, in the chambers of another convent near the city, an abbey under the supervision of Andalucía's most relaxed and liberal abbess, the lovely Esmeralda Purificada (formerly a *marquesa* herself).

19

remedy

"Whereupon your vision blurs and patience fails you in your work, Adela," Milagros had whispered on the night of her passing, "take this. It is a remedy, a potion of old that my own mother taught me. It will fortify your spirits and calm your soul." The feeble teacher had lifted her bedsheet and handed the small brown bottle to her pupil, as she hastily advised in a hoarse whisper, "The contents are written on the back of the bottle. Remember: this is a family recipe that I give only to you, my daughter."

Adela sat before her bedroom window holding the bottle in her hands. She had kept the syrup hidden under her mattress. It was not until this particular evening that the words of her beloved Milagros and the weariness of which she had spoken became relevant. For Adela's eyes were sore indeed. They hurt as never before. Her vision was dull and hazy after working on the most intricate section of the altar cloth; a bouquet of orange blossom. The stitches were the smallest she had ever attempted, so tiny that hardly could they be seen as individual points in each petal of the blossom.

Carefully she removed the cork stopper and sniffed at the contents. Intoxicating scents expanded in the air. Rose petals for certain. And berries. The sweetness of black grapes. Honey, citrus. And something else. A spicy scent. Clove?

She lifted the neck of the glass to her lips and, closing her eyes, sipped twice. A slight burning sensation as the liquid slid from her mouth to her throat. Not unpleasant at all. In fact she felt an enjoyable warmth in her chest. A very good feeling. She sipped yet a third and fourth time.

Then, she lay down on her bed. A rush of heat soon settled upon her cheeks and neck. She felt a slackening in her limbs and closed her eyes. Relaxed, she let herself imagine the future. What would it be? Was she to live a life like this forever? In between freedom and no freedom? Or should she venture out into the world? But how? Whatever would she do without the support of the abbess? And wherever would she live? She was an orphan after all. A child at heart. As she drifted into sleep, she remembered a happy day when she was new to the convent. Milagros had shown her a book in the library, a beautiful book with colored pictures of flowers and birds and little creatures such as snails and dragonflies. She remembered how Milagros's long bony finger traced the shape of a periwinkle again and again, and how she, as a child, nearly succumbed to a trance-like state. So relaxing had that slow, hypnotic action been upon her soul.

A loud braying startled her. Slowly getting up, she patted her skirt and straightened her hem. Then, going to the window, she closed the heavy wooden shutters.

She wrapped a shawl around her shoulders and made her way down the corridor, the stairs, and through the kitchen. Was it Dulzura in the shadows of the pantry whom she saw? And what was she doing there?

Quickly, she rushed to the hermitage and closed the door. The caterpillars glowed like tiny candles. She knelt down to watch as they wove upon the surface of the stones. Then looking at the altar, she caught sight of another tiny light, a drop of glistening amber. It was on the crucifix. She stood up and went nearer. A netting, like gauze, fell from the vertical branch. It was a thing of wonder, this cloth. A strange lace, not unlike a succession of breaths on a cold pane or the filmy morning dew. This was stitchery made entirely of loose loops arranged in an unpredictable pattern, without a recognizable order. But it was pretty, she decided. Pretty for its lack of embellishment.

She carefully lifted the delicate tissue from the cross and removed the caterpillar as well. Then having returned the renegade creature to its diligent army, she left and hastened on to her room.

Once in her cell, she took the cache of caterpillar lace collected over the previous months and sat down on the cot. Ever so lightly she caressed the various examples, one by one with her fingers. Each held a singular design. There were, now, twenty squares with the latest cross piece complete. A few were taken from Milagros's pattern book, but most were of her own invention. A crown of three inches high, a rosette, a galleon. One revealed a lamb and a staff. Another shell, large and whorled. There was an elaborately stitched image of an orange tree. And all of these memorialized events. King Philip's birthday, for one. The galleon was in honor of the Battle of Lepanto. The rosette was a cheer for the abbess's safe return from pilgrimage. And there were letters of the alphabet that spelled *reconquista* in honor of *Los Reyes Católicos*.

These lace pieces were nearly enough to form the border of her altar cloth.

She took from her table the sampler that Milagros had fashioned over the course of her life. It contained one hundred patterns. Inside the cover was a poem written down in her shaky hand. She read under her breath:

> When this you see, remember me
> And keep me in your mind,
> And be not like a weather rock
> That turns at every wind.
> When I am dead and laid in grave,
> And all my bones are rotten,
> By this you may remember me
> When I should be forgotten.

20
heresy

Late in November, just as the abbess had nearly recovered from her wounds, fevers, and jangled nerves, the convent received an unexpected visit from a dramaturge priest, at least the gentleman introduced himself as such to the abbess. His name was Hernán de Vigo Gómez.

On this occasion he was serving the Inquisition; his assignment was to verify an allegation of heresy. One Soledad Paz de García had accused the Saint Margaret nunnery of "witchery and frivolity," in a special council chamber of the bishopric. What is more, she had claimed that one postulant, in particular, a young and beautiful girl named Adela, was "involved with magic and the Devil."

He recalled the moment he was asked to assume this unenviable role quite well, now, as he stood before the convent walls. He had ridden by horseback from Madrid to Toledo to be present at a meeting convened by the High Inquisitors. Upon entering the book-laden library of the cathedral, he had seen three priests dressed in robes of white and crimson. Each wore a simple black mask that covered his face, thereby preventing any guess at his identity. Only obsidian eyes could be seen through cut-out holes.

"Ah, Señor de Vigo," bellowed forth the priest at the head of the table. "Please come forward. And be seated." He motioned to a large chair that was positioned next to a fireplace.

"We have a mission of significant import that requires your assistance. You must not speak of this session with anyone. Not even at court, where we understand you are presently living. Is this understood?"

Hernán nodded. "The bishop of Granada, who is most esteemed among our brethren, has a sister who recently sojourned at the Convent of Saint Margaret in Granada. The purpose of her visit was to find a measure of forgiveness and to seek penance from Our Lord. The stay was to be one month in time, as she felt the degree of her sinfulness to be great. She was hoping to be guided by the sisterhood, thereby finding relief from her guilt. But instead she discovered to her horror that the nuns of that monastery are heretical. She has made several claims against them, claims so strong they must be investigated. Moreover she has identified a sister named Adela as being in consort with the Devil. And if this is verified, we must take action to save her soul. An auto da fé will be ordered. We know you agree that mere death and eternal salvation are better than a life lived in evil. This is a sensitive issue, as the convent has produced great riches for the Church. It is a highly regarded community of lace makers. Even the King has been known to wear their handiwork. And the bishop of Granada feels compromised in the matter, as he too has benefited from the coffers of their monastery. Thus, we need a representative of the Church, such as yourself, under a guise that would never be suspect to investigate these claims. You will act as playwright while you present yourself as priest."

Hernán de Vigo looked up at the sun as he remembered those words. He cleared his throat and, then, dismounted. Taking a rock from his sack—which he used to help weigh down his horse on muddy roads—he knocked upon Saint Margaret's planked door.

Having heard the pounding, Adela went to see who was at their threshold. She peered through the grate and saw a tall stranger. She observed that the man was dressed in worn black velvets, but velvets of rich weave all the same. He was mustachioed and lean. And he carried a large leather bag. Passing a sealed envelope through the opening, he said, "This is a letter from the Duke of Ronda on my behalf. I have matters of import to share with the Reverend Mother, matters that concern the convent and the Court."

"Very well," answered Adela. "Please wait, sir, while I go to her."

After a time, Adela returned with Isabela. Together they opened their door to the stranger, and then Adela instructed Isabela to take the gentleman to the abbess.

As Hernán de Vigo followed the talkative nun before him, he noted the wealth of the convent's furnishings and paintings. Prosperity was evident in every corner of the house. There were painted wood statues of saints lining the corridors. Elegant tapestries adorned the walls. He admired the manicured courtyard with its bountiful lemon trees and jasmine wrapped columns. As they passed through the immaculate garden, richly scented with rosemary and thyme, he got his first glimpse of the Reverend Mother. She stood waiting at the door to her apartment with her hands clasped round a rosary of onyx.

"Welcome to Saint Margaret, sir," she said coughing. "Please do come in, Padre." As the visitor entered the apartment, the abbess motioned to Isabela to stand outside.

After the abbess had made herself comfortable on the sofa, she gestured to the visitor, who in truth looked more *hidalgo* than priest, to sit down.

"And what is your purpose? What exactly brings you to the convent?" asked the abbess. "Have you been sent by the bishop?"

"I come here by request of the Court, not the Church. Let me explain. I have come to ask if I might stage a play in honor of the King for Christmas. It is a piece I have written under the patronage of the Duke of Ronda. In truth it was he who suggested that the convent chapel be the setting for the drama. I believe the duke is no stranger to the sisterhood."

"Yes, that is true. I trust you are aware of our reputation. We are lace makers, Father. And the duke, I daresay, has a weakness for our laces. In particular our ruffs. He owns, I believe, nearly fifty; most of them made by our greatest artist, now passed away. The old Milagros. May she rest in peace. But, please, go on. I would like to hear more."

The abbess adjusted the green satin pillow at her back and looked past the visitor to see that Isabela, while vigilant, was noisily eating an apple.

"The play is to be a celebration of the virtues held dear by Our Lord, Jesus Christ. The nuns will take parts. I will direct."

"Nuns engaged in acts of theatre?" The abbess raised her eyebrows. "Although there are several good musicians among us. And I must confess worthy dancers, too." Here, the abbess pursed her lips. "However, we are an artistic community, to be certain. And if you believe that you might find a way to engage us in your drama, as it were, and if it is really, as you say, the wish of the Court, I will dutifully consider. When did you say the play will be staged?"

"I was hoping the last week of Advent. The King will be in Granada. And the duke is making a present of this production to his Majesty."

"The King himself will attend? I am nearly speechless."

"Yes, Reverend Mother. That is the plan."

"Very well, then. The matter is settled. We are greatly honored, indeed. We will try to please. But you might be disappointed, be advised. To imagine us as capable of playing parts in an act of make believe, well, that is quite beyond us."

"I rather doubt that," answered Hernán.

"And what of your accommodations?" asked the abbess. "Will you be staying with the duke during the coming weeks? Or do you prefer to lodge here?"

"The duke has given me a suite, but an apartment in the abbey would be convenient. I would like to begin rehearsals as soon as possible. With your permission of course."

"Very well. We do have unoccupied guest quarters. They are expressly for the bishop when he visits us and are situated on the third floor, which is very quiet. You may have his rooms. And I shall give you a key to the gate, so you may come and go as you please. Isabela will be happy to assist. And she and Sister Adela will attend to your needs."

"Ah, and one thing more, dear Abbess. I would ask that you not mention to the sisterhood my status as priest. I should like to be known simply as playwright to the Court."

"As you wish, Father."

The abbess stood up and led her esteemed guest to the door, whereupon Isabela showed Hernán de Vigo the way to his rooms.

The following morning Saint Margaret's was rife with gossip. Isabela enthusiastically had begun a chain of tales both true and untrue about the writer in their midst.

"Did you know," she began, as she turned to Hermosa, "that a famous playwright from Madrid is recovering from the dropsy, here? I understand he has come to us by order of the King's physician."

"No, no," answered Dulzura, who was gnawing her way down the side of a lamb shank. "He is a bandit for sure. A robber who will steal our precious laces and make off in the middle of the night with everything we own. Ah, yes. How could the abbess be so daft as to give this thief, however ill he might be, sanctuary. Perhaps he is a murderer, too. Lock your doors tonight, sisters. Be alert."

Victoria looked up from her bowl of milk pudding. "I understand he is the son of the Duke of Ronda. Yes, he is in trouble, but not the kind you speak of, Sister Dulzura. I believe he is in hiding. He has taken a married woman as his lover; her husband is seeking revenge. This is why our Reverend Mother has offered him a room. It is the kindness of her heart not her daftness, as you cruelly say, that permits him safe harbor."

Just then Adela entered the refectory with a platter of crispy *churros* whose golden-brown sheen and deep-fried aroma made the sisterhood swoon.

"We have an esteemed visitor at Saint Margaret, sisters," she announced, as she placed the golden crullers before Beatriz.

"Sister Adela, who is this visitor? Do you know?" asked Victoria, as she grabbed a *churro* and stuffed it in her mouth.

"He is a celebrated writer of poetry and plays. And I understand that he has been commissioned by the Court, the very King himself, to present a Christmas pageant here in our chapel. This is what the abbess has told me."

"And who will act in this pageant. Is this known?"

"Yes. All of us. We are to take parts. Even Beatriz will have a role. And what is more, sisters, the King will be in attendance."

"The King?" repeated the nuns as they looked at one another in surprise.

"Well, yes, Señor de Vigo is, as I said, a playwright of unmatched gifts. He is favored by His Majesty."

And hearing this, Beatriz, who had consumed at least four *churros*, asked, "Sister Adela, may I have some chocolate?"

"Ah, yes, the chocolate. You are, dear Beatriz, in very good stead, as I have been told that our playwright has a weakness for chocolate drink, too. I am asking Isabela to take a pitcher to him now. Yes, you will have your cup, dearest."

21
honesty

On the last Thursday of each month Señor Solá, the wine merchant, made his call at the convent. He was prompt, gracious, and honest, a kindly man who had been a purveyor of libations to the convents and monasteries of Sevilla, Granada, and Valencia for decades. No one, including the abbess, could quite remember how it was that Solá had first appeared at their gate with his little horse-drawn carriage, but that didn't matter. Of import to the abbess was that the merchant offered fair rates for the monthly liters of drink the sisters consumed.

So it was with regret that Adela prepared herself to question the dependable merchant about his recent deliveries. But she had promised the bishop she would do just that.

As was his habit, Señor Solá rang the bronze bell at the garden gate on a rainy afternoon at precisely midday. (He had chosen this particular hour as the provends of Saint Margaret were to his liking, particularly its "rotten pot" of pig entrails and nasty bits seasoned with garlic and hot pepper. And, always, the good abbess would make a little package of cold meats and *empanada* for his journey back.)

Adela, who had been peeling potatoes in the kitchen, wiped her hands on a towel as she briskly walked through the corridor.

Having peered through the little window of the garden wall to identify the visitor, she unlatched the gate, hurting her thumb in the process. She saw that she had torn the skin, just below the nail.

Señor Solá watched Adela as she put her bloodied finger to her lips.

"Good day, Sister." And then, "Is there something wrong?"

"Just a scratch, Señor Solá. Nothing really."

"May I see?"

As he examined her thumb, he took a small vial from his right pocket. "This will help. Let me pour a little on the cut."

Adela nodded. The merchant then dabbed a purple liquid on the wound. "It is a spirit that I make at home from my own grapes. It will cleanse and disinfect. It is beneficial to drink, as well."

"And what is it called?"

"Tears of Boabdil."

She smiled for she had seen this name on Milagros's bottle.

"And why Boabdil?"

"Do you not know the story?" he asked, his forehead wrinkled.

"No."

"Boabdil was Granada's last Moorish king. After Isabel and Ferdinand recaptured the city and took possession of the palace, it is said he traveled south with a great entourage of courtiers and family. They were returning to the lands from which his people and his forbears came long, long ago. Upon reaching a lofty eminence not far from the Alhambra, he glanced once more to look at all that he had lost: the red ramparts of the palace fortress, its lovely towers, the Palacio del Generalife, verdant valleys, fields. And he began to weep. His very own mother, who accompanied him in shame, spat out, 'You do well to weep like a woman for what you could not defend like a man.'"

Nodding as if to say, yes, this is a story worth remembering indeed, Adela closed her eyes and clasping her hands summoned the courage to address the subject uppermost in her thoughts.

"Señor Solá," she started, "I know scant of wine and liquors. I know little of their makers and vineyards. I wonder if you can tell me, please, about the vineyard that produces the wine we purchase here at Saint Margaret. Is it a good one?"

Señor Solá squinted as he listened to the young nun before him. How should he answer, for he knew that there were complaints from others who were drinking the wine from the Jiménez farm. Now, he thought to himself, Sister Adela had not made mention of dissatisfaction. No complaint. No words of rebuke or displeasure. Just a question. Easy enough to answer and, then again, not quite. He knew the Jiménez family well and he knew that they had come upon hard times. And they might have been cutting corners just a bit. Adding a tincture of color to their weaker grape to give it richness. He had even heard that some grape growers were adding pig blood or pomegranate juice, even dye, to their wine. But he did not know that this was true of the Jiménez vineyard. Then again, there were complaints. How to answer Sister Adela?

"Well," he responded, "as to the matter of goodness, I don't know that I can comment. Certainly, it is a vineyard that I have represented for many years. I knew the first proprietor, the grandfather of the present owner, very well. He was a man of dignity and excellent taste. And I have known his son and grandson, who inherited the concern, for quite some time. The vineyard produces several varieties of white and red, you see. It is a large operation, with thousands of hectares. But the matter of good. Well, now, some years yield bottles better than others. So while this year might not have produced the finest of their table wine, too much rain, last year's vintages were quite fine. Very fine."

Señor Solá, then, wiped his neck with a bandana.

"I don't know if you have answered my question, Señor Solá. What I mean to ascertain is whether the vineyard might be less than forthright in its representation of their wine. Bluntly, then, I mean to ask: Do you think it is an honest business. Is the Convent of Saint Margaret getting pure, untainted wine?"

"Ah, well, this is another matter, altogether, Sister," he answered. "I really can't say. But, why do you ask?"

"Because the bishop found it to be suspect at dinner when last he supped with us. He said it tasted sinister. This was his word, not mine."

Might the bishop be too persnickety? He had been told by the baker Molina, just yesterday, that the prelate was impossible to please.

"My friend, Solá, be careful with the bishop," he advised. "Nothing meets His Holiness's standards. He finds unjust fault with my chestnut paste, my apple fritters, and even my *turrón*. He has become a priestly pest. Just wait and see."

Rather than besmirch the Jiménez vineyard or sway to accommodate the bishop's critical palate, Solá opted for a third solution.

"Sister Adela, I have recently begun to market wines from a vineyard in the mountains by the name of Costa. It is a fairly young winery, but it is my opinion that the grape there is good. More than good. Would you prefer to buy from Costa for a while?"

"Yes, let us try this new vineyard. Thank you kindly, Solá. Would you happen to have several liters of this wine with you now?"

"Yes."

"Good, then. We will purchase all you have. And one thing more."

"Yes, Sister?"

"Might I also buy Tears of Boabdil?"

"Certainly. I have two small bottles."

The truth was that Adela had come to like the taste of Sister Milagros's elixir so very much that she had none left to savor. She had even given one of her little bottles to Pilar who was so enthusiastic that she called it "a love potion." All of the ingredients excluding the liquor she could forage from the larder. But essential to the efficacy of the tonic, she felt certain, was this slightly tart-tasting purple spirit.

Finally, Solá bade farewell.

With bottles in hand, Adela went to the kitchen. She collected several lemons, a cup of brandy, cinnamon, dried rose, a thimbleful of honey, an orange, and powdered clove. Putting these provisions in a basket along with the newly purchased alcohol, she hastened to her room.

Taking Milagros's bottle from underneath her mattress, she turned to the recipe:

> Marry one cup of sweet brandy
> with the bitters of a lemon. This union is sacred.

Next, add a touch of jealousy. A whiff of clove,
a wilted rose or two.
The blush of honey. A thimbleful will do.
Orange blossom is essential for this matrimonial occasion.
Last, the bitter Tears of Boabdil.

22

poetry

As the playwright savored his chocolate, which was spiced with vanilla, he thought about the nun who greeted him the day before. There was *un no sé qué* about her. Her allure was distinctive yet hard to understand. For this sister Adela possessed not the perfect profile of the sister Isabela, the one who brought him food and drink, nor Isabela's delectable, tiny-waisted figure. Adela's physicality was pleasing, not remarkable. Neither short and petite nor tall and broad. She was thin with a small bosom. He supposed it was her very purity and, perhaps even more, her unattainability that counted for his interest.

He put his cup on the table, stood up and went to his bed. He lay down and pictured her face once more. It was oval, slightly olive in complexion. The face of a *maja*, an actress. A visage whose features could change to meet the altering moods of a day. Large brown eyes, almond-shaped, with darker lashes still, full black lashes. And eyebrows that tapered to a wisp. Her cheekbones were fine and high, lending a slightly Oriental cast to her prettiness. And she had the smallest, reddest mouth he had ever seen. A puckered tiny pillow of softness. He could imagine kissing those lips well. Her long neck led to what beneath? He wondered if her breasts were fuller than they appeared. And what was beyond those breasts? Gracious hips? There was drama in her presence and something more than that; something that hinted of unquenchable desire.

He reached for his pen and the paper at his side and scribbled down some notes. In order to best use this woman in his drama he must change the script, allowing for her character to shine beyond all others. Yes, he decided, she would take the role of seductress.

Two tentative knocks interrupted his musings.

"Who is there?" he asked.

"It is I, Isabela. Señor de Vigo, is there anything you might need?"

"No, all is fine. The chocolate was very good. Thank you," he answered, amused. "Is lunch served soon?"

"Soon, Señor de Vigo. And today we have lamb roast. Do you like it?"

"Very much."

"Ah, good. So, I will bring a tray to you after the noon hour."

"Fine, indeed."

And then he heard the lovely Isabela sneeze before she said, "*Hasta muy pronto, entonces, Señor de Vigo.*"

He sat down in a large stuffed chair and picked up his notebook. He felt inspired and began his first *canción* for Adela.

The stanza came effortlessly.

> In your name so white
> Paloma
> is the purity of heaven
> and the angels
> angel that you are
> not woman

When he had finished the last line of the third stanza, he took the page and blotted it. Then, he placed the poem in a drawer.

The bell tolled 11:00 a.m. Looking out his window, he saw that the day would be fair. He decided to take a stroll around the grounds, to observe the sisters at their work. What exactly did the bishop's sister say at the tribunal? He looked at the incriminating notes, which he kept in a small black pouch. "The sisters of Saint Margaret are a deceptive order. There is witchery and frivolity in that convent. Most egregious is their passion for the bath. Their ablutions are daily and done in a room of large stone basins. They heat and perfume their water. They love money and only make their lace for the comforts that come with the success of their fineries. They do not praise God as they ought. They are idolaters. A very disgrace to the one true faith. And one among them, the young Adela, consorts with magic. It is believed that she works with amulets and incantations in the hidden darkness of her hermitage. (The nun Dulzura also knows this. It was she who alerted me to this sordid truth.) And . . . I have witnessed this with my very own eyes: several of the nuns refuse to eat ham or bacon. And one more thing. They tried to poison me with tainted wine."

Well, he would see for himself what truths or untruths lay in such accusations.

He reached for his cloak, fastened it with a broach and hastened down the staircase. As he reached the corridor that ran the length of the first floor, he turned left and went toward the refectory. Looking inside, he saw the child Beatriz sitting alone and eating a treat.

"Little one, good morning," he called to her.

"Señor de Vigo, good morning to you," she answered with her mouth full.

A very pretty child she was. Black curly hair fell about her face and large blue eyes evinced intelligence. She reminded him of his niece.

Getting down from her chair, she took her bowl and, taking a spoon of her pudding, she offered it to him. "This is good, Señor de Vigo. Would you like a taste?"

The playwright laughed. "All right, then. Let's have a taste." And he sampled the custard, opening his eyes to indicate his pleasure. "Ah, delicious, indeed. Who made this flan?"

"Sister Adela," she replied. "She makes the best desserts."

"Would you like to take a walk with me, little one? Would you like to show me around the house?"

"Yes, Señor de Vigo." She quickly put down the bowl and ran ahead, looking behind her to see if the playwright would take up the run.

23

rarity

The morning of the first rehearsal for the play was unlike any other morning the abbess could remember. It snowed. Perhaps it was a sign from the Virgin.

As soon as she awoke, she noticed the frost on the windows. She tentatively touched the glass with her pinky and withdrew her finger with a start. It was icy cold. She wiped the frost with her sleeve-covered hand, until a clearer picture emerged of the world outside. The landscape was spellbinding. It was as if clouds and sugar had draped themselves on everything. Under the brilliant morning sun, the waves and mounds of snowflakes sparkled. And snowflakes were falling still. A world of feather down had descended upon them.

After dressing, the abbess hurried to the chapel. Bowing before the Virgin statue, she asked, "Mother Mary dearest, is the priest who comes as playwright here to harm us? Is it he of whom you warned me in the dream or is it another?"

But not receiving an answer on this morn, the abbess slowly walked away, silently reciting her rosary.

Upon entering the refectory, she saw that the sisters were, for once, altogether happy. Everyone was smiling, even Clara and

Dulzura. "Good morning, my daughters," she nearly sang. "And what a morning this is. I am reminded of another extraordinary day at this convent. It happened on the Feast Day of the Name of Mary, September 9, 1320. As told by the ever obedient mother Caridad Renata, the sisterhood had been in continuous prayer from morning to dusk. At first, our ancestral sisters were alerted to a heavenly presence by the sound of angelic chimes in the choir. Light as breath. Pure notes, high and low. Then, before them, above the choir, appeared a pearlescent cloud that spun until the angelic dust begat a thread of golden light. The thread began to shimmer silver. A voice of feminine beauty spoke: 'Sisterhood of Margaret, I bless you, spinners all, and spinners of the word forever, may you flourish.' And then the image of Mary, Mother of God, attended by her court of angels passed over the sisterhood, glistening them with the golden and argentum dust of heaven. For weeks, wrote Caridad Renata, 'the celestial sparkles remained on our tunics, mantles, and our skin.'"

"Mother," cried little Beatriz, "it is white outside, the way the mountain tops look."

"Yes, my little one. It is snow. And isn't it lovely?"

"It is beautiful," cooed Victoria. "A day for celebration. This has never happened before, has it, Mother? Snow on the fields."

"Not that I can remember; no, not in all my days. And what is that you have before you?"

"Mother, Adela has made us snow cups," answered little Beatriz. "Mine is lemon. Juana has strawberry. Clara asked for orange."

The abbess smiled and took her seat. "Well, today should be revealing. Don't you think? Señor de Vigo has many ideas, I understand. Not only are we to take roles in his play but we will also make our costumes."

"Can I be an angel, Mother?" asked Beatriz.

"Angel, my daughter, you already are."

"Where will we learn our roles?" Isabela asked, as she passed a plate of bacon and toasted bread to the Reverend Mother.

"My understanding is the chapel. And we begin soon. Señor de Vigo would like to begin after our late morning prayers."

Adela walked in carrying a small bowl of snowflakes in cream and honey. "This, abbess, is for you. I am making Señor de Vigo a breakfast of ham and our best white cheese. Do you think he will be pleased, Mother?"

"Yes. And cut some sweet bread, too. Would you? The one with the currants."

"Yes, Mother." And off went Adela to tend to her cookery.

Hernán de Vigo stood before the altar in the chapel, waiting for the sisters. They were at the very least, he had decided, an unusual lot. On his walk around the convent compound the day before he had witnessed strange, if not bizarre, occurrences. Unimaginable acts. And, yes, it looked as if magic were evident among these peculiar women. In the garden he had seen the child Beatriz gliding in the air between the columns and trees. Every now and again her feet would touch ground and she would giggle. But no sooner would she maintain contact with the earth than she would be swept up again by an invisible current. It was startling. Yet no one seemed alarmed. The sisters, who were tending to their geraniums and chamomile, snipping herbs and sighing in contentment, acted as though it were the most common of events. They waved and smiled at the child. And Isabela, the lovely Isabela, danced in circles in the garden, never stopping. Round and round as if in a trance, her eyes unfocused.

Having ambled through the courtyard, he walked into the chapel, for the second time that day, to find the abbess feeding berries and biscuits to the Virgin statue. And talking aloud with sighs and *Sí, sí, claro Nuestra Señora*. She might be mad.

But none of these glimpses prepared him for the vision that was the lace room. He stood astonished just outside its doorway. Never had he seen a place of such purity and otherworldliness; its serenity was mesmerizing. Even the air within smelled of an impossible sweetness. He nearly fell to the ground, though, when it seemed the very pieces of gossamer cloth began to fly in the room, taking on angelic forms, and making sounds not unlike the tinkling of chimes.

"Señor de Vigo," he heard from the far end of the chapel. "We are here." The abbess was leading the nuns toward the altar.

Pulled from his thoughts, he looked down the aisle to see his cast of nuns. There were twenty.

Standing shyly before him, they resembled a group of school

girls, even though several of the sisters were clearly very old. As he scanned the faces before him, he caught sight of one that was particularly frightful. Yes, she would play the villain. There were several cherubic creatures in the group and the vixen Isabela. Adela, the seductress. The abbess would be the Virtue Prudence.

"Sisters, please be seated," he ordered.

Waiting until the nuns had sat down in the first two pews, he continued. "Have any of you ever seen a play?"

"I saw angels and a king in our street," said little Beatriz. "There was a princess and a black and red devil, too."

"Good, child." The playwright paused and looked at Adela. "Anyone else?"

The sisters looked at each other, amused.

"All right, then. We, that is all of you, are about to begin an adventure. Something very new for all of you. You are going to take leave of your identities as sisters of the convent to inhabit personages of your imagination. As if in a dream. I want you to set yourselves free, according to my direction."

Isabela stood up. "What does that mean, Señor de Vigo? When you say according to your direction? And what are personages of our imagination?"

Clara laughed and snorted, provoking Dulzura to look cross-eyed at little Beatriz who was jumping up and down in her seat.

"Well, I will make suggestions. Such as, *walk to the right, Sister,* or *smile, please, when you say this bit of verse.* I will assign identities to you and ask that you imbue your sentences with emotion, just like the prayers and rosaries you recite from memory."

"Will there be music and dance?" asked Isabela.

"Between the acts, yes."

"I should like to dance the saraband, then. May I?"

"Yes, and who among you plays the tambourine and mandolin?"

"I do," offered Victoria.

"Very good. And now, sisters, let us begin. Let us sing *Ríu, Ríu, Chíu.*"

Amid the syncopated clapping and the *shake shake shake* of the tambourine was the singsong of the nightingale delivering a message of the newborn baby Jesus.

Later that day, in the privacy and quiet of his third-floor quarters,

Hernán de Vigo thought about the first rehearsal. Had the sisters in truth seemed wanton and free? Were they frivolous and eager to play, as Soledad Paz had so strongly charged? Well, not really; in fact he had found them to be rather shy and fearful of the stage, as it were. And Adela was anything but a witch. She was a virginal little thing, this girl. Not a she-wolf. For sure, they had peculiarities these nuns; particularly the crone Dulzura. And the abbess, most likely, was addled. But nothing heretical, save for a love of music and dance. And were these arts so bad for the soul? He, himself, enjoyed the lute, the violin, and the trumpet.

He jotted down a few notes to himself. But under his breath he uttered, "Careful, careful Hernán."

And, then, he proceeded to write his first report to the High Inquisitors.

24

chastity

Alone in the bathing house, Adela thought about her new role as seductress. Adela the actress. Adela the temptress. But she was Adela *la monja*. Adela the lace maker, the cook, and the helpmate. Until the morning's meeting with Señor de Vigo, she had never heard the word. "Please, sir, what does seductress mean?" she had asked.

Before the playwright could answer, Dulzura shouted out, "She's the Magdalen. The one who brings shame on herself for her passions."

"Señor de Vigo, is that true?" asked Adela, as she blushed and looked down at her feet. "For, I could no sooner play such a part than hurt any one of my sisters."

"Not quite. Not quite. A temptress, Adela," and here he turned to the nasty Dulzura with the sternest expression, "is someone whose beauty is compelling. A temptress can and often does make use of her charms for, let us say, the carnal pleasures, which the Lord has given to his children. To mold men to her needs. But not all seductresses are so shrewd or motivated. In this play, the seductress is a torment to the count. Only because he is besotted by beauty. She does nothing to cause his torment. She is chaste. She simply exists. And in this she suffers, as it is God's gift to her, this beauty, and a curse to the men who desire her." Certainly, thought Vigo, this nun Adela was extremely modest. Concerned about her reputation. A soulful woman. Not the sort to play with magic, as her accuser, Soledad Paz, had blithely suggested to the Holy Office.

Adela looked at the abbess. "Is this all right, Reverend Mother? I am disturbed by this role of seductress."

The abbess was quiet for a while. First, she looked at the Virgin statue, then she thought of Milagros, and finally she gazed back at Adela. Yes, she thought, the description by the playwright suited Adela well. She was beautiful, yet she did not know it. And in the outside world, most surely, she would cause men's torment. But how to answer this child of hers who did not know the world?

"Adela," and she turned to look at all the sisters of her household, "sisters, all of you, we are taking roles in this morality play of Señor de Vigo. There is nothing to fear. We are simply speaking words that could apply to others in the world outside our walls. For the pleasure of the King, remember. It is our duty to 'act' as Señor de Vigo would say in such a way as to make the words seem lively and real. It is an act of the imagination. We must remember that this drama, this work of art, is intended to illuminate and instruct the values of the faith. In this we do our parts quite well, do we not?"

The sisters hummed in unison and looked kindly at Adela.

"Yes, Mother," answered Adela.

Now, lying in the bath, she dared to look at her body in a way that she never had before. She saw that she was firm and formed of curves; broad hips, small breasts. She lightly rubbed the skin on her arms and elbows and decided that it was smooth and soft, even though it daily rubbed against the coarse flax of her garments.

She took the silver container that Milagros had given her in both hands. She had never opened it. "Adela," her beloved teacher had said, "this is soap so rare, so costly, that not even the Queen of Castile has ever known of it. It was made by my father, a perfumer of great distinction. Perhaps even the finest in Granada. Keep it well and safe. And use it sparingly. You will see what merits come from it."

Adela opened the small container to see an oval shape of the palest pink with flecks of gold and azure. It smelled of cinnamon and honey.

And something else. What was it? Taking the soap she slowly moved it over her body. At first she felt a slight tingling on her limbs and stomach, and gradually she was aware of an ever-increasing warmth upon her skin. This sweet-smelling agent in her hand was acting to relax the tension in her arms and thighs, but more than that, she realized that her entire body was glowing with an inner fire, apricot and glistening, like the color of the large opal ring, which the Reverend Mother wore on special feast days.

She suddenly rose from the bath and looked up at the moon. Glancing down at her body, she realized the insignificance of her existence. And, then, as she dried herself with a clean linen towel, she remembered something else Milagros had said, just before she died.

"Adela, should love ever find its way to you, the love of passion, take it quickly. Without reserve. Be courageous. There are many ways to live on this earth; there are many ways to take God into your heart without forsaking that which is natural."

Did she not like this life of quietude and beauty within the convent? Every day was safe and steady, albeit fraught with quarrels. And, among all women, was not the Reverend Mother the most understanding and kindly? Indeed she had tried to make Saint Margaret's a tranquil place of warmth and comfort, delighting in pictures and carpets, flowers and music, good food. The sisters lacked for nothing. So, what was wrong with such a life as this?

And, yet, she had felt something in the very well of her body that she could neither describe nor understand. A yearning.

25

quietly

On a perfect, starlit night, Adela decided to visit the Alhambra once more. Only this time, she would venture inside. She had often thought of the palace as she went about her sewing and chores, wondering if and when she might have the opportunity to visit again. She was worried that she had reached an impasse with her lace work. Though she had progressed with her tableau, if ever so slowly, she had yet to assemble the two parts together. Perhaps she would find inspiration in the Moorish design. She remembered that Milagros had spoken of its honeycombed interior. *The stucco of its walls is worked so delicately as to appear transparent as a veil. The intricacies of lattice crossings, repetitions of form, insistent geometry, are dizzying and inspiring.* She must, she decided, see it for herself.

And so after Friday vespers, on the second week of the playwright's stay, Adela left the confines of the abbey.

The abbess, who had been sipping a goblet of medicinal liquor in her sitting room, heard footsteps as she reached for the bottle a second time and peeked through the window to see the young girl leave. *Hmm, well, this right had been given her. But she feared for her safety. There were murderous thieves about, and worse. She would say a rosary. Ask the Virgin to protect her.*

As she took another sip, she thought she heard more footsteps, albeit of a heavier gait. She looked out the window again and saw that there was someone, indeed—a striking man of imposing nature, in a plumed hat and regal bearing. The playwright.

On his nightly walk around the convent, Señor de Vigo had seen someone, huddled under a cloak, leaving the grounds. Quietly he slipped out the gate and followed after her, but carefully. In the shadows. Who might this be and how did she dare leave the monastery?

As she passed a small plaza where a towering bonfire burned, Adela quickened her pace. Several priests were carrying books from a house and throwing them onto the pyre. From that plaza came human screams and wailing voices from somewhere in the distance. Piercing cries, so pitiful, they made her shiver. Quickly glancing at the scene, she then rushed on, past several houses and a monastery until finally reaching the foot of the hill.

Hernán de Vigo, twenty paces behind, stopped in his tracks. What, he wondered, would a nun from St. Margaret's have at the Alhambra? And how had she even come to know of that old Moorish stronghold? For a moment he considered following her inside, but decided against it: better to wait at the convent for the sister's return. By his art and his craft, he would find his answers and seek his proof. And so he turned back.

Adela nearly ran the length of the hill, so eager was she to commence her business. Passing through the large gate, she proceeded on toward the wondrous palace. The garden was fragrant with age and neglect, thick with perfumes of competing intensity. She stooped to pluck a blossom.

"And who are you?" she heard from a darkened corner.

Adela stood motionless.

"I say who are you?"

Out of the corner of her eye, she saw a tiny old man. Even the bushes towered over him. Dressed in a long white tunic and wearing a white embroidered cap, he approached her with a lantern held high.

"I am a friend, first, sir," she answered. "A friend who comes to do no harm. I come at the bidding of my teacher, now in paradise with God."

"The name of your teacher?"

"Her name was Milagros, and she was a sister of the Convent of Saint Margaret." Adela pointed behind her. "The oldest convent in Granada, sir."

The man now stood before Adela on his tiptoes. "Milagros?" He closed his eyes and said something in a language unknown to Adela. "If this is the Milagros of the family Abenfo, then, yes, you are a friend. Come, come. But first take this." He handed the lantern to her. "I will fetch another."

Adela followed her guide past fountains, several along the way. The first was a tiny mound of stone, out of which grew wild herbs. The design of the planting was haphazard, but also pleasing, as if the growth were a sudden smile at the world and all that it offered. As the water hit the stone beneath, a particular music played. A laughter of a kind. The next fountain was monumental. It greeted visitors with a bow and spoke in hushed music. *Quiet*, it seemed to say. *Before you lies a grandeur of unequalled presence. Pay homage. Be amazed.* And there were freshets aplenty, streaming along gardens of sweet-scented flowers. These led to an entrance, the portal of which was elaborately decorated.

"Come this way, child," he said. "No doubt your teacher Milagros wished you to see this. You may stay as long as you wish. I will be waiting in the courtyard."

Holding the lantern above her head, she walked slowly around the room whose walls and floor were bewildering in their intricacy of design. Above her the ceiling looked exactly like an enormous honeycomb. The plasterwork was rich in golden hues. She looked down to see that the floor held two identical slabs of alabaster, shimmering as pools of milk.

When at last she felt she could remember such details—for she had memorized the elements of form and design that she liked best—Adela walked outside to thank the caretaker, who had finally introduced himself as Hassan, the one and only guardian now of the ancient palace complex. "You may come back as often as you like," he said. "I am here alone, now, to look after the place. No one much cares about the palace anymore. Its glory days are long, long past." And, then, rubbing his eyes, he added. "Your teacher, Milagros Abenfo, you realize, was of a distinguished family of scientists and apothecarists. Her father, Ibn Abenfo, saved many lives among our community. He was the most esteemed man in our quarter. A deeply religious man, a principled man. Did she tell you of him?"

"Very little," replied Adela.

"Well, then, most likely you have not heard the story of the room of perfumes."

Adela shook her head.

"It is said among our people that Ibn Abenfo's great-great grandfather fashioned the Room of Perfumes for the *taifa* of Toledo. It was a special room in the palace, on a high floor, overlooking the river and open to the breezes of that city's hill. And it was from this great-great-grandfather that Ibn Abenfo knew the secrets of oils and potions, as they had been written down and passed from one generation to the next."

"And what was this room of perfumes for, exactly?" asked Adela.

"Ah. Yes. Its purpose. Some say it was for seduction. Others opine that it induced exquisite reverie. This much is known: Those who were fortunate enough to be invited to the chamber would smell of the flowers of paradise until their dying day. Blossoms and herbs of incomparable refinement, gathered from the farthest lands, were blended to make the most exquisite of perfumes. Servants would pour these essences from crystal goblets on the heads and bodies of the kingdom's guests."

The caretaker adjusted his cap, as he closed his eyes.

He continued, "Getting back to Milagros, well, Milagros was like her mother Miriam. A free spirit from the time she could walk. We were the same age, Milagros and I."

Hassan cleared his throat. "I have a story to tell you, if you have the time."

Adela nodded.

Hassan then led her to a bench by the garden path where he beckoned her to sit. As he spoke, the mighty fountain's waters flowed. "Well then," he sighed, "let me share the tale of this most unusual woman. Some say she was an angel sent by God to this earth. She was born on the eve of the Winter Solstice. The heavens welcomed her to the world with portentous constellations. Often our community talked about the sky on that day, the day Milagros came into this world, for it was different, vastly different, from that which they had ever experienced. Even the color of the heavens was singular: pale green with flecks of gold.

"This baby girl had been much anticipated by her parents. A holy man in the community had told them that the child would be remarkable, her form and spirit of extraordinary beauty. A star child. That is what they called her. And that she would converse with the natural world in the rarest of ways. For all that existed would be of kinship to their daughter. She belonged to the universe, and the universe belonged to her.

"When she was born, a small sphere, purple in color, appeared on her forehead. A sign, said the elders, that she was wise at birth.

"She was a pretty infant, or so they say, for I was born in the same year, and what could I have known of such things. The elders talked of her fairness and mirth. Her eyes were of 'a verdant sweetness,' her limbs of 'perfect proportion,' her smile of 'a delicacy unequaled.' Again, I cannot say, for I was just a babe as well.

"But when she was a child of five or six, Milagros began to show her otherworldly powers. She could understand the talk of birds. She read the whispers of the wind. She could describe colors in a rainbow that no one else could see—shades of purity, shades of vanity, shades of pride and honesty. Her elders asked her what such variants meant, and she would answer, 'The color of pride is between the pink and purple bands clear to the eye.'

"Often, when she was very young, she could be found playing among the doves in the early morn. It was as though the birds could understand her childish talk, for often they would gather round her in a circle on the grass. And the smallest creatures of the glen and plain she liked as well. A basket in hand, she searched for winged insects, rabbits, lizards, pups, and kittens. And she liked flowers, especially the poppy and the chamomile that grew thick in these parts of Al-Andalus."

It grew chilly. Hassan noticed that Adela pulled her cloak around her tightly. "Let me serve you tea. Wait. It will only be a minute." And off he scurried into his little caretaker's cottage.

Soon enough, Adela held in her hand a glass of mint infusion. "Drink, drink," urged the storyteller. "It will warm you."

Adela sipped the sweet tea, which made her drowsy. "Sir," she said, as she placed the empty glass beside her. "I fear that it is very late. I wish to hear more of your story. But now I must leave. Forgive me."

"Yes, yes," answered the caretaker, as he peered into the tired eyes of his listener. "But know that you may come back as often as you like to this place. You are welcome here, always."

Adela took the hand of the strange little man and thanking him again, quickly turned away and went off into the night.

26
mystery

The abbess heard the sounds of quickening footsteps. There was a creaking of the gate. And then the final click shut. It was midnight. She looked out her window and saw that Adela had returned.

That night the abbess found it hard to sleep. She worried about Adela. And then the wind blew strong, the moon was too bright. She felt at odds with herself and the world. Even sad, but why she could not say. Sometimes she felt this way. There was something, too, about the playwright that festered within her. She had learned from several of the sisters that Señor de Vigo often walked the halls when everyone was in bed. Indeed, Isabela had seen him hovering near the hermitage entrance, trying to force open the door. While she consoled herself with the knowledge that he was in the service of the duke and that she herself had freely given him accommodations, she had not expected him to roam about wherever he pleased, like a spy. Should she confront him, and, if so, to what avail? She would maintain a friendly disposition. And at the same time she would say very little. Somehow, she couldn't quite trust this priest, if priest he truly were.

Taking a key from the rope around her waist, she unlocked a

small chest in her sitting room. Rummaging through its contents, she removed a letter, a velvet cap, and a book bound in leather.

The abbess went to her chair, now, lighting the oil lamp beside her. Carefully opening the small book's cover, for it was crumbling with age, she read the inscription for the hundredth time:

> For my dearest daughter Adela. May your find your history and destiny in the truth of these pages. Your loving mother, Sara.

Adela, too, looked through a manuscript that unusual evening. Taking Milagros's pattern book in her hands, she studied the pages toward the back. There it was. A pattern she had thought peculiar upon first seeing it, but now not quite as strange. She noticed that there were at least ten more of such designs on the inside of the back cover. All of them were florid. She studied them with interest. Inherent in their strategy was an element she had not perceived before. A kind of script, perhaps. Stitches that were foreign to her eye and familiar at once, as these were the stitches unique to Milagros's lace. None of the sisters could replicate them, though try they did—for it had always been Milagros's particular lace patterns that were most sought by nobility and the clergy. Was the pattern a language? Yes, she recognized these patterns as the arabesques on the stucco walls of the Alhambra. She remembered now, "On each and every piece I sew, I leave a prayer to Allah."

27

nativity

Señor de Vigo stood at the front of the chapel, awaiting the cast of sisters. He was deep in thought, for the day before he had received word from the bishop that his sister, the pious Soledad Paz, was in an abject state. Why had he not moved forward in his investigation? Did he not understand how much she suffered from the slowness of his work? She was teetering on the edge of salvation. She had made her claims. Now he must support them with his proof. Did he not have news for them? The bishop ended his letter with a warning. "I expect to have your complete report on the day of your drama's presentation. You can give it to me then. For I shall be in attendance with my sister."

It was the hour of the first dress rehearsal.

The child Beatriz entered before anyone else. Running and moving her arms wrapped in wings.

"Señor de Vigo," she cried out. "I am an angel."

And not only did she move as an angel, thought the playwright, but her face, her form were nearly more cherubic than the putti he had seen in countless cathedral ceilings in Madrid! This child was indescribably ethereal.

The sisters came in twos and threes, often smiling and touching the fabric of their simple costumes with appreciation. María, though plump and fleshy as rising dough, even felt pretty. She was the perfect heavenly cloud in her snowy cotton cloth. The abbess, by contrast, in her robes of simple and stiff muslin and sack, seemed the very essence of her character, the noble Prudence. Dulzura wore a mask of midnight blue.

"Sisters, sisters," boomed Señor de Vigo, as he clapped his hands twice. "You are a remarkable cast. The duke, the court, will be impressed. Even amazed."

Meekly they stood in a semi-circle around him. Not daring to lift their eyes to the director, for they felt shy. But they were also excited by the prospect of performing for the King at the most precious season of the year. The Nativity.

And where were the beauties among them? Isabela stood shyly at the back, as did Adela.

"Let us start," began the playwright, "with the opening lines of Virtue Prudence. Abbess Ana please step forward, here."

Señor de Vigo pointed with his right hand to the statue of the Virgin.

The abbess slowly walked with a cane to her place. She looked around her, admiring the stage scenery. The pride and affection she felt in that moment for her children made her heart swell. She surveyed the chapel, its vaulted white ceiling painted with little gold stars, the *azulejos* on the lower walls, the polished terracotta floor. She loved the chapel more than any other room, for it was where the voices of the sisters were lifted up to the Virgin and the Holy Trinity, each day. A room of exultation, praise, and song.

"Our King most noble and his retinue and all the personages of royal blood among us," she clearly said with a flourish of her hand, "we entreat you to enjoy our humble play."

"Good, good," cried the playwright. "Continue on."

"Virtue Prudence am I. The narrator of our story. Listen well and learn of the mercy of Our Lord."

Hernán de Vigo directed the Reverend Mother to stand back by the altar, in the darkness, while he motioned to Beatriz to flutter across the dais.

"Little Beatriz," he intoned with more warmth than was his custom, "might you flutter even fainter, as though you were a feather on the wind?"

Beatriz looked at the abbess for a sign of approval. With the nodding of her head, she grinned broadly. Putting out her arms and squeezing her eyes in concentration, she began to slowly lift off the floor, a few inches at first, but then she rose still higher until she was floating a full meter above. "Like this Señor de Vigo?" she asked, looking down at him.

The playwright stared in awe, just as he had done the first time he witnessed the flying child.

"She is blessed, Señor de Vigo," said the abbess, as she motioned to Beatriz. "She has found favor with Our Lord."

"Indeed," answered the playwright. "And, now, for the music. Victoria, step forward, please."

Victoria, dressed in white and bearing a golden halo around her head, began to play the tambourine, while singing:

> Such golden meadows,
> and green fields
> around this house of prayer and solitude
> with riches in abundance
> the grape
> the rose
> and honey
> are for your royal disposition.

"Please, Isabela, dance!" ordered the playwright. "And continue on Victoria!"

Isabela twirled until she was overcome with dizziness. And then the scene in which she was a part became blurred. The playwright, the Reverend Mother, Beatriz, and all the others were transformed into bands of color, presented like a rainbow. Could it be that she saw Señor de Vigo touching Sister Adela's waist?

28
regality

The day of the theatrical presentation had arrived, and there was not a sister among them who felt confident or well enough prepared to meet the King.

As Adela rushed around the halls and passageways of Saint Margaret's, helping Isabela put their house in sparkling order, she heard the commotion of people arriving in the courtyard. Peering out the kitchen window, she saw the bishop and his scowling sister, who was still dressed in mourning weeds, stepping from their carriage.

The abbess appeared and the three began to walk toward the cloister.

"I wonder what they're chattering about," said Isabela as she used a feather duster to clean the pantry. "Most likely the bishop's sister has acid on her tongue. What a nob."

"Let us forget her for the moment, dear," answered Adela. "We must finish with our chores and get dressed quickly."

Soon, Adela and Isabela, wearing simple shifts of muslin and cotton masks, were waiting with the other sisters in the refectory. Beatriz was twirling round; Clara was clearing her throat with a hideous cough; Dulzura was making faces; and Victoria was straining to sing her lines in a voice as high and light as a canary.

The abbess appeared at the door.

"My children," she began, "the King and Queen are in their honored seats. The bishop and his sister are in the pew behind them. The Duke of Ronda is here with his retinue. They look glorious, dear children. The King is dressed in gold and silver. The queen is wearing scarlet and rubies." She closed her eyes momentarily. "Are we ready to begin?"

"I am terribly frightened," cried out Victoria. "Mother, I don't know that I will be able to sing once I see the King."

"Child," answered the Reverend Mother, "remember that we commemorate the birth of Our Lord with this presentation. We must do our very best."

Adela went to Victoria and patted her arm. "Dear, do not worry. All will be well. You shall see."

And then Hernán de Vigo appeared behind the abbess.

"Sisters," he intoned, with a graceful, courtly gesture of his hands, "the moment has come for us to show the King and Queen what we have accomplished. Let us go now to the chapel."

Immediately following the end of the production, the King began to clap ebulliently. Had he ever been so enchanted by displays of fancy and delight? He had reveled in this most enticing pageant. And such a venerable cast. He applauded, too, the employment of animals of the field: donkeys, roosters, sheep, and lambs. The wispy clouds of silk, rich velvet banners. *Deus ex machina*!

He lost no time in arranging to meet each sister. The two young postulants, Adela and Isabela, had impressed him in particular for their simple beauty and chaste demeanor. "Would they take their vows?" he inquired of the abbess, as he stood admiring the two. And she had answered, "Perhaps, perhaps not."

When Hernán de Vigo approached His Majesty on bended knee, the King bellowed his enthusiasm and complete delight.

"Señor de Vigo," and here he clapped once again, "you must write another of these remarkable plays for the Court. Might you compose a special drama for Saint Margaret's that I may attend on Holy Week?"

And then, just before the King was about to take his leave, he walked up to the Virgin Mary. So arresting was the immanence of her form, that he found himself staring at the statue's perfection throughout the pageant. He allowed himself the pleasure of stroking the Virgin's velvet gown; he noted her exquisite white lace mantilla, the refinement of her visage. It was, in fact, a perfect effigy. A most beautiful work of art.

Two
1579

29

festivity

It was the New Year. Festivity, nearly ecstatic—if the sisters were to allow themselves such freedom of emotion—was in the air at Saint Margaret. The drama had been a wondrous success, indeed. And for this the abbess and the sisters were grateful. The King was very pleased with such a show of veneration. But this was not an altogether welcome development. "How," they asked the abbess one night at an especially elaborate supper, "will we be able to make our lace and also participate in another of Señor de Vigo's plays?" They had lost precious time already in such a theatrical pursuit. They were behind on their commissions. Their lace work waited, and their clients were impatient. "Why, just yesterday," advised Victoria, "the Duquesa de Alba sent a messenger demanding that we finish the baptismal gown for her goddaughter. What are we to say? That we now are players? No longer makers of lace? Might this not sound frivolous?" And then María added, with more irony than could possibly have been imagined, "What of our reputation?"

"Well," answered the abbess, "it seems that the bishop is in favor of our doing these plays with Señor de Vigo. He has written to me of this new work. He even asked that it be dedicated to the Virgin."

The sisters looked at one another, raising their eyebrows and clucking.

"I know," said Isabela. "Perhaps fewer of us can be involved in this Easter pageant. At least some of the commissions might be completed on time."

"But who shall decide which of us will act?" asked Victoria.

"I shall, with a bit of counsel, I suppose, from Señor de Vigo," replied the abbess with the weight of her authority. "Yes, Isabela, you have offered us a good solution," she decided. "I shall put the matter before him tomorrow. But let us now enjoy this lovely dinner that Adela has prepared for us. And praise be to the Giver of all tasty things!"

The meal was perhaps the most sumptuous Adela had ever conceived; this was owing to the fact that the duke himself had made a gift of special foodstuffs to the convent. Shortly after Christmas, a servant bearing a letter of gratitude and two large baskets had come calling. The letter explained that the partridges, fruits, nuts, and libation were from the duke's own estate. That the duke himself had felled the birds. The persimmons and pomegranates were from his orchards. The Marcona almonds were of the highest quality, both sugared and salted. And the sherry, of which there were four bottles, was so highly prized that the King himself ordered two cases of the liquor each year for his private cellar.

And the abbess's generous brother had sent an extravagant shipment of foodstuffs, along with silver trinkets, from his city in the New World, too. Among the precious comestibles were potatoes of extraordinary color, blue and yellow, purple and rose.

Perhaps no one else feasted as enthusiastically as little Beatriz. She had also been drinking the duke's special libation.

"Little Beatriz," cautioned the abbess, "you may eat as many almonds as you like, but you mustn't drink the sherry."

"Why, Mother?" she asked as she hiccupped and then began to laugh.

"Oh, dear," said the abbess wincing. "Isabela, did you not notice the child has been drinking sherry?"

"Mother, little Beatriz can be quite stealthy," announced Isabela. "Especially when it comes to sweet drinks, of which she has a monumental fondness. I am sorry. No, I was not watching her as I should have been."

The abbess had, by now, gotten up from her chair and gone over to the little girl. Taking the child's face in her hands, she smiled and repeated, "Beatriz, you simply cannot drink this."

But the abbess was finally incapable of admonishing such an adorable, angelic presence who had brought so much joy to everyone; the child was favored by God, after all. "Now Isabela," the abbess said, "will take you to your bed. All right, my dear?"

And, with that, little Beatriz dutifully let herself be swept up in the sister's arms, but not before she shouted, "I have had a vision, Mother. Someone dear to us will be swept away!"

The abbess, looking startled, replied, "Dear, dear. The sherry. Too much sherry for such a tiny child." Then, turning her attention to the others, she quietly announced, "And, now, my daughters, I must excuse myself. Please remember to come by my apartment this evening for the annual giving of gifts."

But what had the child predicted? Was a calamity about to descend upon them, and if so, could this be true?

30

agony

Soledad Paz lay on her bed in a state of agony. Her anger and growing frustration over that interminable investigation had reduced her
to a wreck. She was certain that her own soul was in danger of eternal hell if she failed to prove her claims.

As she reached to scratch her head, she thought she felt a worm.
No, worse than a worm, a snake uncoiled in her hair. Dear God. Was
Lucifer upon her? Oh, the thought of such damnation. She bolted
upright and ran around her room. Thoughts of demons, their fangs
about to gnaw her flesh, her bosom, bottom—for of course they
would find the juicy bits—tore at her brain.

That foolish, foolish playwright. What kind of investigator was
he? No doubt he had been beguiled or bewitched by the young Adela, a crafty one, after all. Hadn't she seen with her own eyes the convent's sisters pursuing both gluttony and lust? Wasn't it the devil's
own lair? Oh to imagine such things! Clara and the bull! So much
glorious food? The disgust of it . . . no doubt the abbess was one of
those witches too.

She must do something. She must. For having witnessed such

evil made her an accomplice to Satan. Unless of course she could rid the earth of those malevolents.

And then having worked herself into a frenzy, all the while drooling onto her Bible, she collapsed into a faint, face down upon her bed again, in a catatonic state.

31
epiphany

Later that night, the abbess met with the sisters privately. It was an annual custom: A Three Kings Day observance, in which she gave a token of esteem to each and every nun. She had labored over these small gifts. For María, she had made a small cross from the polished branches of a lemon tree. To Victoria, the most musical among them, she gave a pair of castanets fashioned from shells found during her pilgrimage. Most difficult had been deciding on a present for Dulzura. After months of pondering the matter, the abbess had chosen sweets. Perhaps, she thought, more sugar was needed in her diet, for her humors were sorely out of balance. And so she had made candies of date paste and honey, which she molded into tiny hearts. For Clara she decided on a garland of dried roses to replace the strands of garlic that she forever wore around her neck. She had written poems and prayers for most of the others. For the frailest Inés, however, a new shawl of velvet was in order, for Three Kings Day and the sister's saint day were the same. And then there was Adela. She had decided, come what may, the time was at hand: she must be given her inheritance. The young woman would finally have in her possession the letter, the book, and the cap. Thus, would she confront her right-ful heritage, however confounding it might prove.

"Adela," cautioned the abbess as she had handed her the book, "remember that what you read in these pages and who you are might not agree. You must reconcile yourself with your life as it is, not as it might have been. I shall say no more. This bestowal, from your mother, your blood mother, must be savored and taken into your heart. With time. And when you are ready, perhaps I can talk to you of what I know. All right, then?"

Adela received the gifts of the Reverend Mother with trepidation and excitement. For finally, after all these years, she owned some-thing of her mother and her origins. "Abbess," she said, her voice breaking slightly. And then she had stood up. "May I go now?"

"Yes, child."

But instead of going to her room, as she had intended, she found herself walking about the convent and, eventually, the cloister. Fi-nally, she sat down on a bench and stared into the darkness. Would these objects in any way guide her?

She felt chilled, for the air was cool.

Listlessly she stood up and walked to the kitchen, holding her keepsakes in one arm. Noticing a basket filled to the brim with sweet oranges, she took one, inhaled its scent, and made her way up the stairs.

As she reached the final step, she halted with a gasp. For there was Señor de Vigo standing in her path. She turned away.

Smiling, he grabbed her with both arms.

"May I pass, sir?" she asked in a whisper.

"You may not," he said, laughing. "And do you really want to, my little one?"

Then, bringing her close, he kissed her mouth. A kiss so sudden, so unexpected and greedy, that Adela let herself respond in kind. She could still taste the brandy on his tongue, as she ran toward her room.

Closing the door, she stood against it with her heart pounding: She felt excited and embarrassed. She had been offered a kiss. And she had willingly returned it.

32

lucidity

What to do with the information she now possessed? She read for the second time the twenty-third page of her mother's book. She stopped when she came to the thirteen principles of faith on which her mother wished to guide her: that divinity creates life; that He is only one; that He is incorporeal and unchangeable; that He is eternal and above time; that it is a duty to obey Him; that all the words of the prophets are true; most particularly the revelation through Moses; that it is a duty to believe in the Law; that the Law can never be changed; that God is omniscient; that His retribution is just; that the Messiah will come; and the resurrection of the dead.

Overnight, everything she believed to be true about herself was challenged by these things in her lap: a book, cap, and letter. And among them, the letter was most troubling, for in it was the story of her parents' lives. Grim details of being denounced as heretics and taunted by neighbors. Of friends turned enemies. Of her family made to prove their "purity of blood" and having their possessions stolen by officers of The Holy Office. Her grandparents had disappeared without a trace. Her little brother wrested from her father's arms by a priest.

She could not stop thinking about her parents' fate. What had become of them? The cruelty of her history seemed no more reasonable to her than the snuffing out of a babe's breath.

But there was something more to the letter, at the very end. A few lines written in a very careful hand.

> Daughter dearest.
>
> All I truly wish for is your happiness.
> Live your life by loving. Someday marry. Have children.
> Thus, our family will live on in you.

She picked up the cap and looked at it carefully. It was old and of an elaborate stitch work. Silk and velvet, light gray in color, and embroidered in white and blue threads. As she turned it over, she felt its pebbly lining, as if there were stones sewn within.

Getting up from her chair she went to her basket of notions and took a blunt needle. Then carefully, ever so carefully, she pulled at the seam until the rent was wide enough to allow the contents out.

Gently she shook the cap. There were stones, indeed. Like chips of ice. Some were square and others round. One was large as a grape. Carefully she wrapped them in a piece of cloth and placed them in her basket. "These are the few things that your mother brought with you," the abbess had confided on Three Kings night. "I did not ask for explanations, Adela. She said to give them to you when I thought it best."

33

delicacy

Hernán de Vigo, feeling somewhat gleeful by the prospects of a romantic adventure and a prolonged stay at the convent, met happily with the abbess, at her request, to discuss his plans for the new pageant. They sat in the courtyard, where the morning sun shone white upon verdancy. Doves were cooing. A light breeze rustled the lemon trees.

The abbess studied the playwright's face. What was he thinking, this Señor de Vigo, priest and playwright? And why did he seem particularly animated of late. His eyes were fiery, more fiery than ever. And there was a swagger to his walk she hadn't noticed previously. What was he up to? Isabela had told her that she found him in the cloister with a lantern the night before.

He kept turning the pages of a notebook, while clearing his throat.

"Señor de Vigo," began the abbess, "I wonder if I might ask the following of you. But, first, let me say how honored we are by the King's interest. To perform once again for the Court. Please know that we will make every effort to surpass our first attempt on the stage, as it were. But, and I think you will understand my concern, we have our lace. We are behind in our work. Therefore I ask that a smaller number among us be given parts. In this way, at least some of the sisters will be able to pursue their commissions."

The playwright answered quickly. "Yes, yes. Of course, abbess. I understand. Might I make my own choice as to whom?"

"That depends," she replied. "Certain sisters have specifically asked that they not take a role in your play."

The playwright thought for a moment. Pulling at his moustache, he said, "Very well. But I would really hope to include the postulants Adela and Isabela, the sister Dulzura, and the child Beatriz."

The abbess smiled. "For reasons I may know?" She looked down at her hands and felt her palms begin to sweat. Her heart was racing.

No, thought Hernán. But he replied, "Well, I think they have talents that may be of use in this new pageant. Reverend Mother, would you like to listen to a line or two of what I have composed thus far?" he asked.

The abbess nodded, as she squinted her eyes.

And at that, Hernán de Vigo stood and recited from his notebook. Not long. Perhaps five minutes, but long enough to give the Reverend Mother a sense of his vision.

"Above all else, Señor de Vigo," she began, "I wish for you to understand that the tribute you have written must be measured from the heart, for no one can communicate with the Mother of God without true devotion."

Upon hearing the abbess's admonition, Hernán stood up and bowed. And thanking the dear Abbess Ana for her time, he went back to his room to begin the composition of what he hoped would be his best morality play. Yes, in honor of the Virgin, he would pen this work. But in many ways the play was for Adela. In most ways, truthfully. She was his inspiration and his muse. She would take the part of the Virgin.

Maybe Adela was a true love, not passing fancy. Their secret kiss had proven the truth of sex, yet once again. It was the fundamental engine. The flame of everything that mattered. This young and enchanting nun, whose virtues went beyond the obvious, was a cauldron of unexplored desire. She was creative, too (essential to good lovemaking). There was delicacy and imagination in her cookery, whether roast of lamb or suckling pig, omelets or orange cake. Her recipes, he had discovered, could cause delirium in a man. Even now the remembrance of her sweet rice pudding made his mouth water, the intoxicating aromatics of cinnamon, vanilla, cream, and honey. Yes, he could eat a potful of it at this very instant. Any accusations of her "witchery" could be boiled down to natural talent. For she was no accomplice to the devil. In fact, if anyone was Beelzebub's handmaiden at Saint Margaret it was Dulzura. Of this he was quite, quite certain.

Taking an extravagant plume, he began. The first line of the play.

Virgin:
Feast upon my milk and honey, my honor,
my glory. The tears I shed for my Son's death,
true diamonds of heaven.

The milk and honey of Adela; the matter of what was on his mind. He longed to see the rosy flesh of his new love, which was under all those folds of coarse, drab cloth. A nice, taut belly, a virginal waist, he was certain, was waiting to be devoured. He closed his eyes and imagined Adela in the nude, lying on a bed of satin, her arms outstretched to him.

And then the moment of ravishment. Her legs about his. He dipped his pen into the inkwell and continued.

Virgin:
I am pure before all others, and suffering long. But praise in song
Our Father, Son and Holy Ghost, all morn and evening long.
Our King and Queen, most noble
The majesty of this land
Attend with us
Observe in prayer
this Holy Week
of sadness and of grief.
Come, come
And hear the story
Of our suffering Christ and Lord
Redeemer, creator
Omnipotent
Ruler, ever more.

Angel:
Hear the lute
the mandolin
Hear the bandurria
Viola de Gamba.
Shhhh. An intruder comes!
Who is it?

Intruder:
I have come to feed you
berries red and dear
I have come to clothe you
Golden dress,
and silver sandals.
Hear my prayers for mercy
Hear my prayers of thanks
Hear my little heart beat
Holy Mother sweet.

Now for the voice of Dulzura. He rubbed his hands together. A villain of some sort. A fallen angel, demon, some creature not quite human, with her disturbing eyes and ugly mouth. Perhaps a malady. A cause for suffering and grief? Ah, yes, the affliction of Envy, devouring her own heart. The perfect fit.

Envy:
I have come to show you
what you do not know
I have come to vex and foil
all that you might do
For I am a weakness
an illness
of the soul.
Behold
a night in a convent of
Toledo.

Angel:
Hear the bell toll
twelve. It is midnight.

Virgin:
In this holy week
all must share my pain.
Do not seek good food or wine
But vinegar and herbs
and holy water
for our penance pure.
And ask Our Lord for protection
against all evil.

The playwright got up from his desk and poured himself a glass of red wine. A good start, he thought. And now it was time for a hearty lunch. But, first, he must write to his overlords at the Holy Office. He now had more detailed information for the Inquisitors than that which was related in his preliminary findings. He would forget the bishop and his nagging sister, though. Enough of those two incorrigible nuisances. His obligations were elsewhere.

Smirking, he took his pen and began the salutation of his report with:

> Most Honorable, Exceedingly Noble, Gracious Executors, Magnificent Overseers, Venerable Graces:
>
> After several months I do have news for you, but perhaps not as incriminating as the charges against Saint Margaret seem. For while there are peculiarities in this house, among them a near obsession with a statue of The Ever Virgin Mary and a mysticism that is hard to fathom, at least for me, your most humble servant, I find that I cannot verify acts of heresy among this sisterhood as yet. And therefor I beg to have more time to study carefully that which the sisters might be hiding in the darkest hours of the night. . . .

34
reality

"Well, your mother was dignified," said the abbess, as she passed a tiny cup of sherry to Adela in her private sitting room. "You might wonder what I mean by this. She inhabited grace. She was tall and elegant. Your mother's features were refined. And she had very blue eyes."

The abbess paused. "Adela, this is difficult for me, more painful for you to hear. Dare I go on?"

"Yes, please, Abbess. I wish to know about that morning."

"Your mother was holding your hand tightly, so tightly that I worried she might hurt you. She let go when I held open my arms and beckoned you to come to me. But before parting, she gave me a sack and told me that the contents were your inheritance. And that you should receive them when you entered womanhood. All these years I have kept the articles within a chest."

"And anything else?" asked Adela, as she looked down at her hands.

"Yes."

The abbess stood up and went to the sideboard. Taking a pear, she cut it and arranged the halves on a plate with a slice of cheese.

Then, slowly, as she turned around, she walked to the table. "Eat, child," she said. "You haven't eaten."

Looking down at the floor, she continued, "Adela, you are different from the others at the convent. You came here as a child, just as most of your companion sisters, it is true. But not the same."

Adela remained silent.

"Do you remember anything of your childhood? Anything at all? A nursery rhyme, a song, a toy? Something of the house in which you lived? Something of your father, perhaps?"

"Nothing, abbess. Except, and this is vague, a sound memory, my father singing. Singing something to me."

"Well, perhaps, this song was in a language different from our own. I might venture to say not *castellano*."

"Why?"

"Because, Adela, you are of Hebrew lineage. Your parents were *conversos*. Christians . . . but of *sangre judía*."

Adela looked at the abbess as if she didn't understand.

"But, Reverend Mother, how is this? How do you know this?"

"No sooner had I let you in Saint Margaret's door, your mother whispered in my ear these things." And then she added, "Your mother and your father were fleeing from the Holy Office."

"But I am Christian, am I not, Reverend Mother? Am I not a child of the Catholic faith?"

"Yes and no," answered the abbess quietly, with a slight smile.

"Adela, you must search your heart to find the answers you seek. I love you as I love the others, save for Dulzura. I cannot, I confess, find the measure of compassion in my heart for that woman. I sin in this, I know. But this is the state of affairs." The abbess crossed herself before continuing on. "But you I truly love, my dear. And what I wish to remind you is this: Love disperses darkness. And in this vein, I ask you to think about the wants of your own heart. For I do not believe your mother wished for you to live the life of a nun against your will. It is for this reason that I ask you to carefully consider whether or not you desire to take your vows. Think hard about it. For, you may stay here all your days, without the vows, remember."

The abbess stood up. "And now I must attend to the Virgin's dress. I urge you to pray, child. Pray to understand what you find difficult to comprehend."

After the abbess left the refectory, Adela went to the lace room.

Entering the space, she saw one new, exceptional piece in progress, hanging from a pole above her head. It was a sash, a most beautiful one. Half-complete. And Victoria, she could see, was working the finest silver thread into the pattern in the most subtle of ways. A whisper of color. For a most dashing count, no doubt.

After sitting down, she closed her eyes and let her fingers trace the latest pieces she had completed.

So silken, so fine was the *lacis* of the first piece that she felt not the slightest change in relief among the many worked into the elaborate parts. She had employed five different stitches in its composition, which depicted Milagros as a child. Her image figured at the center, surrounded by the tiny creatures of the wood she adored. There were snails, rabbits, little birds, a squirrel, and deer. So perfect, so fine was this lace that it seemed not of her own hand.

The second piece was in honor of her mother, the mother who now inhabited the world of an altar cloth, not only her daughter's memory. She had sewed a constellation of stars in her very own stitch, which she called "the celestial stitch." There were thirty in all, large and small stars. Interlocking in circles so that they appeared as one. One star of glory.

And the third piece, smaller than the others, was of a heart, her own, which she depicted in three kinds of threadwork; Mezzo Mandolino, Ruedas Sol, and appliqué. This piece of heart lace, as she thought of it, had been initiated the morning of the snowfall. While scooping up a bowl of ice for her confections, she had seen a pattern on a drift that resembled a heart; no doubt a track of a rabbit or squirrel. But there it was all the same. And within its contour there had been more patterns; some glazed with ice and others not. And as she had stared at this marvel of nature, she thought to recreate the template in her own hand. The stitch work was among the smallest she had ever attempted; so miniscule that her eyes teared while she sewed. Still, as she observed her work, she saw that it was good. This pleased her.

But, now, what of her Hebrew heritage? And what did this truly mean? Would she forever be a worker of lace inside the confines of a monastery? Never a true nun? Who exactly could she be?

She turned the pretty pieces of her craftsmanship over and over again, absentmindedly, as if to find the answers to her past and the reason for her existence in the intricacies of her handwork. Then, she looked at her fingers. Were they, she wondered, in the shape of her mother's and her mother's mother. Had her mother sewn as well? The world was suddenly an endless stream of questions without answers. Only guesses and images of her imagination.

35
homily

When the bishop finally understood that he had little sway over Hernán de Vigo and that the playwright was working according to his own measure and conscience, he decided to placate his sister as best he could with a little homily and scripture each day.

Not wanting to return to Toledo for she feared the demons of guilt would overcome her there, she had taken residence in a house next door to his own, a house owned by the Church for distinguished guests of the prelate. In the garden of her new abode, the bishop counseled Soledad Paz in matters of faith.

"Dear Sister," he would say, "you trouble yourself needlessly about the Convent of Saint Margaret. Let the Inquisition do its work. Righteousness will prevail, my dear Sister. And, you will be comforted to know that I have sent yet another damning letter of the convent's behavior to The Holy Office. I have told the Inquisitors to act expeditiously, without favor, to purify the order of its corruption."

But Soledad had nearly lost all sense of decorum, her nerves having gotten the best of her. Sometimes she would howl all afternoon. And then by some unknown force of energy, she would begin to talk incessantly about the riches of Saint Margaret with frightful disdain. The idolatry. The fineries. And the wealth of those ungrateful, hateful nuns. She reminded her brother of the tapestries on their walls, the little bulls of silver on the tables, the rich and exquisite food, the wanton ways of the girls Isabela and Adela, their games of magic, the gluttonous child Beatriz, the horror of it all. "Why," she would end her ranting again and again, "don't you think that they are filling their coffers with riches that belong to the Church? Where does this gold and silver come from? Their laces, Brother!"

Often, upon leaving his sister, he found himself exhausted. He wished the whole affair would simply go away. Maybe, by some miracle, it would. One thing was certain, at least. He had decided to give the acreage of Saint Margaret to the monks of Saint Ignacio. For years they had wanted those fields. Well, now, they would get their wish. Bit by bit he would strip those evil nuns of all their status and wealth.

36
ability

The playwright sat in the parlor of his suite, turning the pages of his play. How to get his cast of players, nuns of reserve, to better interpret his words and the emotions they conveyed; this was the problem. How to teach these women to act?

Of the four, little Beatriz was the most promising; she feared nothing and followed his directions without quarrel. And she possessed a natural ability, a flair, for singing and dance. Favored by God? Perhaps. The levitations were a sign, no doubt, of some ability to escape the bounds of reality. But she had something more than a mystical gift. She was, he was certain, an artist at heart. Were she not a child in a convent, he would apprentice her to Agata, his former mistress and amor.

Getting up from his chair, he paced the room, rubbing his chin in thought. It was Dulzura who posed the most curious dilemma. She was necessary to the production, for certain; she added the touch of drama that was sorely needed in the action, but she was impossible to direct. Ugly, yes. Wicked, maybe. Unfeeling. This was the problem. She seemed to be void of mercy. Or if she did possess a heart, it might be better likened to stone. He must try a new approach with her. What would Agata say, he wondered. "Hernán, Hernán, play the lover, which you play so well." Yes, he could hear her saying this. "Woo her with your charms, love."

Well, were she not the form of an old she-goat, he might be able to woo. But how to seduce a woman so coarse of face and dead of soul? "Ah, Hernán," Agata would say, "you, my love, are the master of seduction. Make her into something wonderful. Write her face. Write her form. Make believe. Acting is believing. Isn't that your line?"

Ah, Agata. He missed her; there was no denying it. Missed her fetching form and golden hair. Her aquamarine eyes. He hungered for the silk of her skin, the feel of her embrace. Her passion. Her sex. Her bed. Yes, indeed, the sadness, joy, and ecstasy, the exhilaration and desperation of her bewitchment.

He poured a glass of brandy and drank it down.

There was a knock on the door.

"Yes, who is it?" he asked.

"Isabela, Señor de Vigo."

"Yes?"

"The sisters are waiting in the chapel, sir."

"I'll be there shortly, thank you, Sister."

He waited until he heard the nun's receding steps. Then, the playwright donned his black velvet cape, took up the unbound pages of his drama, and left.

The little group of sisters was waiting shyly. Adela still beguiled, though. And he noted she was blushing. What, he wondered, were her feelings toward him? Amorous as his? As he stared at the group, he began to undress Adela in his mind, yet again. For the fortieth time? At least. He was certain that her bosom was rounder than her dress allowed. Were her nipples dark as Agata's or fair or blush. Large? Small? Buds or blossoms. How would she smell? Musty or sweet.

"Señor Hernán?" shouted Beatriz.

The playwright suddenly came back from his libidinous reverie. "Yes, little one."

"Are we to begin?"

"Yes. And let us begin with you."

The playwright gently took the child by her arm and placed her on the landing near the altar. "Now, Beatriz, dance a *chacona*, while you shake the tambourine. Then sing out the line, 'Hear my tale of long ago and take heed of my story!'"

Beatriz did exactly as she was directed and added a special flourish at the end, a curtsy to the statue of the Virgin and another to Christ the Lord.

"Well done, well done," the playwright said, while laughing. "And now, Dulzura. Do you remember your lines?"

"I will try," she answered. "But I'm not feeling that well, sir. I have eaten something disagreeable for breakfast." She looked down at her feet. Then, quickly looking up and rubbing her stomach, she added, "I have rotten eggs."

Out of her mouth came a sound of such wretchedness the others heard it as the dying whine of a mule or the wail of a sow giving birth. All were certain of its odor: as vile as Dulzura herself. Of a fume and fury so sharp that Hernán de Vigo fell, hitting his forehead on the holy water font.

Rushing to the playwright's side and kneeling down, Adela asked, "Señor de Vigo, are you hurt?" She noted the bump on his head. "I will fetch some water. And a salve."

Then getting up she brushed against him, just enough to confirm his suspicions of her voluptuousness.

Later that day, after their rehearsal, which the playwright thought had gone quite well, better than hoped for, he met with the abbess to discuss the setting for the Easter pageant.

"Abbess, I have a special request to make of you."

"Yes?"

She handed her guest a plate of biscuits. "These are quite good. Made this morning. Adela's cinnamon snaps."

Hernán de Vigo put one in his mouth, savoring the pungency and crispness of the pastry.

"I would like to stage the Easter play, this time in the lace room."

The abbess narrowed her eyes. "And why is that, Señor de Vigo."

"For its rarified ambience. A perfect backdrop for the allegories of purity and charity. I could not help notice that the room is ethereal, Abbess. Inherent is the light, first. A radiance inhabits the space. And the beauty of the lace, its softness and intricacy, imitate the very clouds of the celestial kingdom. When a zephyr enters the room, the pieces sway and move in beguiling fashion. It is a mesmerizing *corral*, if you will."

"Yes, indeed. It is second in loveliest to the chapel. The heart of our community." She closed her eyes and made the sign of the cross. "Let me think on this matter."

"Thank you Reverend Mother. And now I must get back to my writing. I have nearly finished the third act."

"Very well. And please look after your forehead. I see you have a nasty bump there. I will have Isabela take a compress to you."

"Thank you, Abbess. Thank you."

After he had gone to his room, Hernán de Vigo decided to make some music. He picked up his violin and played at random, creating a lively little composition. And as he fiddled, he thought about the progress of his notes for the Holy Office. Thus far, he decided, he had seen no witchcraft, devil worship, or frivolity. Adela was no "handmaiden of Beelzebub." She was a sweet thing, a juicy little sweet thing, who could do no harm to a fly. Was there love of music, love of dance at this nunnery? Well, yes. The passion of Isabela. He had never seen a woman dance as well or often. Whether *chacona, mariona, pabana, zarabanda*. She was gifted of a rhythmic understanding. And the abbess was a bit zealous in her devotion to the Mother Mary. But this was hardly a crime. Although he found it bizarre that she conversed with a wooden statue, fed an unyielding mouth fruits and sweets, and changed the Virgin's dress every week. As for Clara. She was pure peculiarity. Sour-smelling, too. But she seemed devoted to her work and meditations. It was Dulzura who presented the reason for wonder. She was nasty. Good for drama, but problematic for a convent he supposed. With a flourish of his bow, he played notes befitting the depths of doom and sorrow. Dulzura. Was she the well of discord? The embroiderer of mischief and intrigue? He would pay attention. Keep track of her ruminations and discover her secrets.

37

secrecy

Adela had not been to the hermitage in days, so busy had she been with household chores, her cookery, thoughts about her mother, the ministrations of the playwright, and the *comedia's* rehearsals.

At dusk, one night, she hurried to the little hut, carrying a bowl of mush. She found that the door to the hermitage had warped, making entrance impossible. But after pulling hard at the latch and kicking the bottom beam, she was able to release it.

Crouching as she entered, for the door was low, she peered within. The caterpillars were nowhere to be seen. No longer did their golden bodies sparkle in the darkness. No longer were they clinging to their stones.

Adela rubbed her eyes. For what was this? A halo of iridescent moths encircled her, moving slowly round and round, until each landed upon her person, shyly fluttering. Lacy rosettes. Shimmering stars. She put her hand to one and felt its silken skin, so light. Would her touch be harmful? And then, just as mysteriously as they had appeared, the winged angels took leave of her, one by one. They danced about the hermitage, first, in a perfect triangular pattern. Then each abandoned its position until in linear flight they slipped away, never to be seen again.

She stooped down to examine the lace that was left and found that it was of a superior quality than that which the creatures had made all year. Finer, more silken, and of a cast that literally glowed gold.

Gently taking the lace pieces from the stones, she wrapped them in her apron and hurried back inside the convent house.

No sooner had she left the cloister garden, than Hernán de Vigo stepped out from the shadows. Quietly, taking especially long strides in soft kid slippers, he approached the hermitage. Pulling on the latch, he crouched low to enter. Within were the simple walls of a humble hut, bare, save for a crucifix. There were stones on the ground. And one thing more. What was it? Bending down he found a scrap of luminous cloth. It was, he realized, a tiny piece of intricately woven lace.

38
especially

As soon as Adela entered her room, she lay down on her bed, holding the exquisite caterpillar work in her hands. She closed her eyes and thought about the playwright. Especially his form and voice. She blushed to admit: she loved his voice. It was of a teasing sound, not quite deep, but deep enough. A voice that caressed and eased her sadness. As if the voice could smile. Was this the love of which Milagros spoke? This constancy. For she thought about him every hour of every day. Another secret in her life of secrets.

She took the first example of the caterpillar lace and realized that the shape was round, not square as the other lace pieces had been made. And within this oval shape a simple flower. The lily. Yes, she remembered having drawn the lily with her brush and olive oil. But this lily was particular. Inside the petals was the stamen, long and gold. How had this been sewn, this gold? For it was a marvel. Just as Milagros had said, "The Alhambra caterpillar lace astounds and confounds. It is of a complexity and beauty unattainable by our human hand. Behold it and, in gratitude, thank God for its existence. For its mystery will never be solved."

Now she spread the squares on her bed, trying for a pleasing pattern, looking for harmony. Holding up a candle to better see the tapestry, she detected something else about the lace she hadn't noticed before. Each creation had a pocket sewn to the back. For what reason?

Finally, Adela gathered the lace and put it on a chair. Then, she removed her shift and slippers and fell into bed, but not before saying her prayers. And this night, her prayers included an extra concern. Her aching for the playwright. She ended her meditation aloud with, "Strengthen my resolve. Forgive me all my weaknesses. In Jesus name I pray. Amen."

But even though she was tired, she could not sleep. She stared at the ceiling, said the rosary twice. Tossing and turning, she became ever more agitated. A thought occurred to her: the problem she was having with the altar piece was simply one of the imagination. Her refusal to let the matter be. Reticella, Gros Point. Very different stitches. Yes. Incompatible, perhaps. But might not opposing stitches be joined? Yes, she would let them fall together. In natural effect.

And, then, she heard a sound at the door. A quiet tap, tap, tap. She stiffened. Not a movement. Not even a breath. And then again a tap, tap, tap. Her heart beat faster.

"Adela. It is I Hernán. Please open your door."

Against all dedication to the principles and virtues that the sisterhood had taught her, Adela got up from her bed and calmly walked to her destiny. She let the playwright in.

Shy and forward at once, she led Hernán to her bed and allowing him to remove her nightdress, she closed her eyes. She felt his lips on her neck, her stomach, and finally her breasts.

After he had reluctantly left her, Adela walked around in circles. She touched her lips to find that they were swollen. Hernán had been bold, and she had found that she too was an insistent lover.

As the playwright made his way down the corridor—his passions aroused in a way that not even Agata compared—he thought he heard a cackle. And not quite human. Then, just as he began to bound up the third floor stairway, he caught sight of the noisemaker. Dulzura.

39
piety

The King was in his castle study in Madrid, listening to his architects droning on about their latest projects. The new Escorial palace monastery was near completion. The advisers in his midst were arguing for yet another monumentally expensive wing, an addition to the grand salons and corridors, library, living chambers, and chapels, to house his most glorious works of art, the finest sacred art in the land. As he listened to their flowery language, and their fawning epithets, and "Excellency, Your Majesty, Gracious Benefactor," he spotted two turtle doves outside his window. Two pretty little puffs of perfection. And their image reminded him of another duet, that of the little nun doves of Saint Margaret, the young girls Isabela and Adela.

His wife, the Queen, had need of more help did she not? Ladies in waiting and such. Would not those girls of piety be perfect maiden servants? And lovely to look at for the men of his palace. For his own eyes as well. For he did appreciate the female form in its multiple varieties. Yes, he must write to the abbess Ana and make his pleasure known. Those lovely, dewy girls with those big black eyes. So sweet they were. And willing servants of God. And subjects of his rule.

"Your Grace," asked the Treasurer, "are you with us?"

40
royalty

Only the day before, the abbess had received a letter that troubled
her greatly. It had arrived by courier directly from the King himself.
Among the issues pertaining to his imminent visit was news of the
Queen's growing household and her request for two dressing gowns
in Point de Venise. The main part of the letter, however, concerned
the new royal residence at El Escorial. It was the King's all-consuming
passion at the moment. He wrote in detail about the growing monastery and the assembling of a household staff large and competent
enough to serve such a monumental edifice. He wondered, if perhaps, any of the sisters might make the sacrifice to join the royal
household. He remembered two quite exceptional nuns whose obedience and manner he found worthy of the royal assignment. The
sisters Isabela and Adela. They would, he opined, add sobriety and
excellence to the royal retinue.

But paramount among his concerns was the royal treasury and
the furnishing of the new chapel. Advised by the court artist, who
was traveling to Venice quite often of late, unusual sculptures of the
finest craftsmanship were increasingly hard to locate. He had been

searching in Florence and Toledo for statuary of brilliance. In particular, images of Our Lady the ever Virgin Mary.

The abbess was holding this letter in her hands. Alone, in her sitting room, by the light of an oil lamp, she stared at the sentence that read: "It is my express wish that the Convent of Saint Margaret offer the Virgin statue of your chapel to the Chapel Royal at El Escorial, as an act of obeisance and humility before Your Lord and Sovereign, God Almighty, the Church, and the Queen of our land."

41

savory

"Daughters," began the abbess one evening at supper, "we have much to discuss concerning the repast that we are to offer the King and Queen after our Easter pageant. A matter of great importance. And of sensitivity. The food that we prepare must be of the rarest taste and quality. Who among you would like to offer ideas for the menu?"

"I suggest we make capon with almond sauce," answered Clara, first. "I can remember that Milagros used to make this succulent meat often. We all enjoyed it, immensely."

"Do you remember the ingredients, Clara?"

Clara scratched at her temple, to relieve an itchy rash. "I think the sauce was of raisins, peppers, and parsley. Perhaps a touch of rosemary." She scratched at her temple yet again. "It was wine sauce. Red wine! I remember now, yes. Delectable. Not like the fatty meats and gas-making broths we eat these days." She scowled at Isabela. "You, Isabela, might have learned how to make this dish had you not been so stubbornly insistent on plying us with those disgusting testicles and terrines. Adela's cookery, at least, has healthful ingredients. And her sweets are quite good."

"Now, now, Clara. That is quite enough," scolded the abbess.

"Can we have flan?" asked Beatriz. "Flan with natilla, Reverend Mother?"

"For dessert, yes, little one. But let us consider the main dishes first."

"Meat balls with olives and prunes. I adore meat balls," gushed Victoria. She started to giggle. "And ham croquettes. Oh, we must have ham croquettes, Mother."

"I have a thought," said Isabela. "A turkey! Let us make a turkey stuffed four times. First with herbs of rosemary and sage. Olive oil and walnuts. This mixture goes underneath the skin. Carefully, the skin must be pulled from the flesh to be a kind of purse for these condiments. Then one must cut around the legs. Deep cuts which are to be filled with bits of old bread and raisins, prunes that have been soaked in wine. Just a bit. Now for the garlic and olives. This is mixed with a ladle of honey until a kind of paste forms in your hand. Slits are made in the breast of the meat and filled lightly with this stuffing. The breast must be sewed closed, so as not to let the juices out. Does this not sound grand enough for our King, sisters?"

"And what is the fourth?" asked the abbess, as she drooled ever so slightly.

"Apples and oranges in the cavity, Mother. Very simple. Cut-up fruits to keep the turkey moist and tender during the roasting."

"This dish is elegant," said Adela, as she squinted. "Yes, I believe we should offer turkey to the King."

"Do we not cook capon, then?" asked Victoria.

"I think," the abbess answered slowly, "that we are better represented by a feast with turkey as the main course. Capon has a lovely flavor, we all agree. But the complexity of this turkey dish is fitting for such a special occasion. And, now, what ideas might you have concerning rice and greens?"

"Almond rice, Mother," Dulzura replied, as she pricked Clara in the arm with her sharpest sewing needle.

"Ayyyyyy," shrieked Clara. "Dulzura is up to her old ways. She just needled me." And then hitting Dulzura in the arm, she added, "I loathe you, more than loathe you, Dulzura."

The abbess took sternly to the malevolent exchange. "Whatever are we to do with you, Sister? Must you always be the booby? Go now to the chapel and prostrate yourself before the crucifix. For an hour, do you understand? And here is the whip. You know what to do with it."

Dulzura made a face at Clara and quickly left the others, mumbling under her breath, "Speak of the devil."

The sisterhood resumed their conversation without further mention of that vilest of women, if woman she truly was.

"I like cod rice," blurted out María. "Remember Milagros's cod rice? Rich with saffron and peas."

"But what of sweet rice, Mother? Adela's pudding rice is my favorite." This, the opinion of little Beatriz.

Old Inés then spoke, as if being stirred from a deep sleep. "As for greens," she said slowly in a trance-like stupor, "I like spinach. Spinach and chickpeas." Rubbing her wrinkled hands together and closing her eyes, she began to mumble under her breath and abruptly sang loudly:

> Cocido, cocido,
> delicioso cocido
> espinacas y garbanzos
> bordado por tocino
> chorizos enormes
> pedazos de cerdo
> aceitunas y papas
> cocido, cocido,
> dulce cocido.
> ¡Ay como me encantas!

The others smiled politely, but the abbess fearing for the poor nun's fragile mind, motioned to Isabela to take the ancient to her cell. "Let us continue thinking about this dinner," she said, as she got up from the table. "And now I must retire to meditate on other matters." And with that the abbess solemnly left.

The abbess knelt on the floor, her hands clasped round her rosary, and prayed directly to the Virgin. How, she asked the Heavenly Mother, could she part with that statue of her after all these years. Had not the image of Our Lady been the centerpiece of everything at Saint Margaret since its founding? Did not the convent's chronicles detail all the miracles ordained by the Virgin Mother herself at this place of prayer? Was not the Virgin carried to the convent by a pilgrim two centuries earlier, a pilgrim whose very words to the founding abbess Theodora were, "The Virgin asked to live among you always, as a sign of favor to the nuns of this sacred site."

One by one she pondered the miracles that the Virgin statue had wrought, both long before the abbess's birth and the miracle making at Saint Margaret's that had taken place during her own years at the convent, beginning with the story of Hermengilda.

She closed her eyes and remembered Hermengilda. How she had suffered from all manner of infirmity. Wracked with the angriest of pain in her chest, her waist, and all four limbs. She, herself, had tried with Milagros so many times to heal Hermengilda. They had applied powders and potions, syrups, hot stones to her skin. A physician had bled her. Nothing had helped. And then one day while she had been feeding the Virgin a sweet roll, Our Lady began to speak. "Go to my daughter, Hermengilda," she had ordered. "Place your hands, Abbess Ana, on her temples and speak my name. She will be left of all pain. Go now and do as I say."

And it was so. Hermengilda that very day, long near death, was healed of her afflictions.

And then many years before, there was the Day of the Immaculate Conception, when she was only eight and newly arrived at Saint Margaret's. During the singing of Veni Creator at matins, all of a sudden the air in the chapel became sweet with carnations. And then the miracle, the first her eyes had seen: carnations, pink and red, began to fall from the ceiling, everywhere. Was this not the handiwork of Mary, Mother of God? Oh, but they were about to take her away: What should she do?

The abbess decided to go before the Virgin and ask her for an answer.

Standing in front of the beloved statue, the abbess made her fears and sorrows known. She implored the Heavenly Queen to help her. *How should she answer the King?*

After reciting five Ave Marias, the abbess heard the Mother of God speak clearly and with majesty. But although she understood the words, each and every one, the abbess was startled by the Virgin's answer. For believe it she could not.

42

calamity

One Sunday evening—exactly a week before the King's much await-
ed second visit—after the sisters had gone to bed and all the lamps
had been extinguished, after each and every prayer and supplication
whispered had made its way to heaven and the angels, saints, the
Virgin, and the Holy Trinity, they began. The rains.

So life-giving and necessary to the nurturing of flowers, fruits,
and trees in springtime, the rain fell softly upon the fields around
Granada. "The mercy of the showers," as the abbess was wont to say,
whenever the April skies broke open to weep.

Isabela, in her cell, remembered how the sound of rain always
lulled her into a peaceful sleep, as if she were surrounded by kindness
and the promise of blessed renewal. . . . Rain. Lovely rain, thought
Isabela, as she drifted off into wonderful dreams that Lenten night.

Little Beatriz, also felt wonderment, but at the furious thun-
derclaps that came rolling through the darkness toward the mountains, and always followed by a flash of lightning. Up out of bed, she
stepped barefoot on the *pres dieu* to get a better look. The rain was
falling, falling.

Adela, too, was marveling at the omnipotence of the showers that night. Did the Lord ordain this rain, she wondered, to wash away the sins of the world? To purify the land? To remind His children of His power, however he might choose to show it?

She stood completely nude, for Pilar and her stories of passion and lovemaking had convinced her that the body was a marvelous thing, something in which to rejoice. For her wide hips, the rise of her breasts were given by God. And she liked the way she felt without a tunic or mantle.

She opened the window to let the freshness of the night air in. And rain began to fall upon her body, making her skin glisten.

It was then that she heard a tapping.

No mystery visitor, for she knew the rhythm of the knock. There was Hernán outside her door. Dressed in a gray silk robe.

Without a moment's hesitation, he, as if under a spell, pulled her close and they kissed. And then the playwright, having made up his mind, led Adela to her bed. Holding her waist, he entered her deliberately and slowly. And Adela, surrendering to the enormity of his passion, responded with abandon, allowing the playwright to do whatever he pleased with her. (For him, a wonderful surprise.) If his tongue sought her breasts, so be it. A bite of her neck. Yes, yes. His hands explored her every curve. And the rain continued on. It rained, that night of nights, with the force of a hundred waterfalls. Determined. Constant. It fell upon the fields and valleys, it fell upon the rivers and oceans, on vineyards and towns, as the lovers reveled in their pleasure.

By the time Hernán left in the early hours of the morn (thrilled by their amorous doings), Adela was so spent by his energies that she fell into a slumber so deep and welcoming that the banging at her door did not, at first, awaken her. When, finally, she heard the cacophony of screams and cries beyond, she got up with a start. Quickly slipping into her tunic, she raced to open her door. "A flood, on the first floor, Sister Adela!" cried Isabela. "It's terrible. A calamity."

Putting on her cloak and slippers, Adela followed Isabela down the stairs to the courtyard. As they passed through the cloister, the two women saw a great rush of water coming forth from the sanctuary. So swift was the current of this deluge that it knocked the sisters down, half drowning them. Adela's slippers disappeared in an instant. Grabbing on to the doors of the chapel, the two women looked within the darkened space to see that their beloved room of worship had become a lake, a great pool of dirty water, upon which floated a disagreeable stew of weeds, branches, and foul-smelling vegetation.

Every pew was submerged. But worse was the absence of the beautiful Virgin. She had vanished.

Adela had lost her grip when another dank stream pushed her toward the convent baths. As she strained to stay afloat, she finally got hold of a column. With a great deal of effort and a silent plea to Saint Jerome, she righted herself. Shouting to Isabela to stay strong, she added, "I'm going for help."

Then, she pushed her way into the convent proper to find the sisters scurrying about and praying.

The abbess, whose dress and habit were drenched, calmly came forward, joining them.

"Children, the Lord tests us. Go to the lace room and await me there."

"Mother," began Adela. "The chapel is flooded. Come see. And Isabela is in need."

"Show me, Adela," she answered. The abbess moved slowly, as the rain had seeped into her very marrow, nearly crippling her with pain.

The two nuns left the interior of the convent to find Isabela, shivering, walking toward them.

"The current has passed," she muttered in shock. "But, look, Mother it continues to rain."

"Yes. We must go to the lace room, now, my daughters. At once."

When the three women entered the convent's workshop, they saw that the others were unabashedly weeping.

At first, neither Isabela, Adela, nor the abbess noticed the damage to the walls and ceiling, the floor, and windows. Their eyes, perhaps miraculously, were averted to such material destruction. All they saw was the suffering of their beloved family.

But, gradually, the three saw that the sisters before them were crying into their arms. Or rather into the great mounds of soiled cloth in each of their arms.

Adela, squinting, wondered at such odd, brown vestments. But, then, looking above her, she saw that every piece of lace had been swept away. No gentle garments of snowflakes and stars overhead, anywhere to be seen. And then she looked to her own table, where she had carefully kept her altar lace work. She could see none.

"The lace, Mother," cried out Victoria, in sobs. "Our lace, Mother. What has become of our beautiful lace?"

Falling to her knees, Victoria spread out tenderly the sole garment she had managed to retrieve from the deluge. A muddied bridal veil, ripped and torn to shreds. A work on which she had labored for two years, and for which she was going blind. It was, without doubt, the most elaborate, finely patterned garment of the tiniest bouquets and open stitch work that she had ever made. So taxing had the execution of the fine-pointed sewing been on her health, that she could no longer stand upright. And her fingers had become deformed.

Just then as the abbess held the distraught Victoria in her arms, Hernán de Vigo walked into the lace room, his eyes searching for Adela. As soon as he saw her and it was clear that no harm had befallen her, he addressed the gathering.

"Sisters, I will make an inspection of the convent. And abbess, I suggest, respectfully, that you and the sisterhood go to the refectory for something to drink, to warm yourselves. I have passed through the room, and it is dry. At least for the moment."

"Yes, yes, you are correct. Let us do this, sisters. Some chocolate, perhaps, will fortify our spirits."

With bowed heads and muffled cries, the sisters, holding the spoiled lace pieces to their breasts, followed their cherished Abbess Ana as she began to lead them in a Te Deum.

That sorrowful day as the early morning hours led to noon and, finally, dusk, the rains began to stop. By supper, they had ceased altogether.

From sunup to sundown, the playwright entered each room of the convent to assess the extent of the damage. Most ravaged were the chapel (which he immediately noted was empty of the Virgin statue), the lace room, and the first floor cells, particularly those belonging to the sisters Clara and little Beatriz. The kitchen, too, had sustained injury, especially the ceiling, which was falling down in chunks of stone. As he walked from space to space, taking in the enormity of the loss, he began to notice that a kind of *mugre* was appearing everywhere. So extensive and far-reaching was this abomination of decay that he wondered at the meaning of it. For was this not a sign of wickedness? On the walls, the ceilings, the precious paintings, red curtains, and velvet-covered chairs. Insects, of a manner grotesque, were feeding on the miasma of growth. And an odor coming from the mold permeated the air. The mold had grown so quickly. Too quickly, he thought. Was this the work of the *diablo*? His eyes would not stop watering. His temples began to throb. He wrapped a piece of cloth around his mouth and nose, as he continued on with the unsavory business of inspection. When he finally had finished, he felt heavy of heart. How to tell the sisterhood that their house was a ruin of huge proportions and treacherous to all. For what was once a sanctuary of beauty and safety had suddenly become a heap of cobble immersed in fetid air.

It was the time of vespers, and in the refectory, thankfully still dry, the sisterhood had gathered in silence.

Unable to visit the chapel, for it was in such a disastrous state of mud, mold, and vermin, the despondent nuns sat around the abbess as she tried to uplift their hearts and comfort them through prayer.

Adela, who had carefully ventured into the kitchens with Isabela, had prepared a simple meal of cheese, sausage, sardines, and olives for the community. And she had brought out jugs of wine to warm the mood. While some were eating, others drifting off to sleep, the playwright finally appeared with his report.

"Abbess and sisters," he began, "the state of the convent is grave. And I believe that all of you must leave at once. For you cannot sleep in this air, so thick and rank that I, myself, can hardly breathe."

The abbess then spoke. "But Señor de Vigo, where can we go in this hour of the night? It is late. And we are tired."

"I will go by horseback to the Duke of Ronda," he answered. "I will ask for his help in the coming days. But surely there must be another abbey that can offer beds and provisions tonight. Again, I insist that you leave this place."

Adela, then, turned to whisper something to the abbess.

She was certain that the gatekeeper of the Moorish palace would help them.

When each sister had collected her most precious possessions and gathered in the refectory, the abbess spoke these words: "We will go to a place of peace, sisters. And we will rest. And the Lord will guide us. I am certain."

And then the sisterhood and Hernán, who had insisted on escorting them on their little journey, bid the convent farewell by making signs of the cross. The abbess locked the gate behind her and with her daughters went forth into the darkness.

43

hostelry

The abbess and Adela walked side by side leading the others in a serpentine line led by Hernán, gallant as always, on horseback. They moved slowly, as the roads were thick with mud and strewn with debris. Now and then the abbess squeezed her young charge's hand in thanks for her companionship.

When they reached the path that followed the hill toward the Alhambra, the sisters stared in wonderment, for they had never beheld such a marvelous sight.

They passed fields of wild herbs, chamomile, and poppy, which in the aftermath of the rains, endowed the air with pungency and freshness. And when, at last, they reached the Gate of Justice, Adela went ahead.

The sisters, although sad and weary, nevertheless wondered at Adela's daring move. For it seemed that she knew this place. How?

Dulzura seemed giddy with a dark knowledge, in the back of the line. Now, this pretty nun of trickery would reveal the truth about her love of magic, she thought. And Clara started sniffing about her, looking to see if the others seemed to notice Adela's familiar manner with the playwright. But no one said a word. They were beyond weariness and in need of sleep. And hopeful that Adela could secure hostelry.

And this she did.

Returning to the bedraggled group, Adela beckoned the sisters with a turn of her hand. "Come, come," she said.

It was, then, that Hernán addressed the abbess. "Wait here, at this place, Reverend Mother, until I have returned with news from the duke. Hopefully in the morn." And with a tilt of the brim of his hat to his amor, for he suddenly realized, smiling to himself, it was Adela, and not he, who had seduced the other, Hernán galloped away.

One by one the sisters solemnly passed through the gate to see that Adela and a tiny man in flowing robes and sandals were gathering lanterns, ten in all, to aid them in the darkness. In pairs, the sisters took one lamp each and followed the abbess and her favorite. They walked past fountains and lush rose gardens to a courtyard, beyond which lay a magnificent alcove.

"We will sleep within," advised Adela. "This kindly man, Señor Hassan, will attend to us."

Within short order, the gatekeeper came to them, carrying bedding. After rolling out the thick red carpets on the marble floor, he bid them good night.

But before submitting to an overwhelming exhaustion, Adela felt an urgent need to speak privately with the abbess.

"Reverend Mother," she whispered, as the abbess slowly bent to straighten out her carpet, "may I have a moment with you?"

"Yes, my daughter," she answered wincing, as she stood up in a corner of the room. The two nuns walked outside to talk in the courtyard.

"Mother, you have not said a word of Our Lady Virgin. She has left us."

"Yes, Adela."

"But, Mother, can you tell me what has happened."

"She was taken by the storm."

"But mother, where has she been taken."

"I do not know. But, it was our Virgin's will. She herself ordained it so. And, now, my child we must sleep. Let us go inside."

44

hospitality

The following morning, when the sisterhood awoke to cock cries in the distance, they drifted out the door and saw that the morning sky was apricot and golden. And it was warm. Hassan had arranged a generous breakfast for them, on small copper tables, in the courtyard. There was *tortilla* of the freshest eggs, sweet onions, and thinly sliced potatoes, drenched in sharp green olive oil and salted to perfection; little rolls that were warm and dense with fragrant cardamom; thick slices of quince. Pitchers of juice.

As the sisters sat under the morning sun, they ate and drank with gratitude. Beatriz played with a bunny that was busy nibbling weeds near a fountain.

The Reverend Mother was the last among them to awake, but when she did, she delighted to see her children seemingly at peace and reveling in the day's good humor. For not only were her children eating with enthusiasm but they were also laughing and telling stories from the Bible.

"Do you remember, Sister Inés," began Victoria, "how Noah and his wife and family survived *their* flood?"

"Of course," answered Inés, as she took a bite of bread and jam.

"And do you remember how Noah stood high upon the ark and blew the ram's horn and started to dance with his wife so that all the animals would follow them. And the animals danced, too!"

"What are you saying, my dear Victoria? That is ridiculous!" And all the sisters, nodded in agreement.

But, then, Isabela stood up and said, "It is true. Sisters! Noah danced like this. Look!" And she began to move her hips under the radiant sun with her arms outstretched, singing "*Gracias, Señor, gracias por su bondad*."

Adela smiled, gently shaking her head. For Isabela never seemed to have a care in the world. Even in such distress, thought Adela, Isabela could find a way to distract herself from the worries at hand.

When the abbess saw that everyone had finished with their breakfast, she beckoned them to assemble around her. "Now, my daughters, let us spend the day in prayer and meditation, asking God for guidance."

She led them to a hall adjoining the alcove where they had slept. Each and every sister kneeled upon the hard stone of the floor and, in perfect silence, offered up thanksgiving.

Finally, at dusk, the abbess led them in a spirited kyrie.

It was then that Hernán appeared before them, accompanied by the dwarfish palace caretaker.

"Sisters, I have good news. Very good news. The duke is sending carriages tomorrow to take you to his palace until the bishop finds a way to house you in a more suitable fashion. I have been told that the bishop will inspect Saint Margaret's soon, to determine what should be done."

Later that night, as the sisters warmed themselves by a fire that Hassan had built in the garden, the sisters looked around them at the miracle of the Moors, the Alhambra. This palace could be "a home in heaven," Isabela kept repeating aloud. "Why, look at its design," agreed María. "As if nature and house were of the same composition. This place is even more beautiful than Saint Margaret's." The women hummed in agreement. "This is a blessed place," said the abbess, "because it has offered us shelter and peace. And what is more, the Lord led us here through Adela. Let us forever remember the kindness of Señor Hassan."

And at that the sisters crossed themselves.

45

strategy

The Duke of Ronda, a man in middle age, was an aristocrat of particular and exquisite tastes. This the sisters knew. For not only was he admiring of their finest, dearest work—and paid them handsomely for it—but he was generous and thoughtful. Over the years, he had sent special gifts of food and delicacies to the monastery for special saint days and anniversaries, for Christmas and for Easter. And knowing of the abbess's fondness for delicate plants and flowers, he had also offered her the services of his gardener to help her plant an elaborate bed of various herbs and florets.

But the sisterhood could never have imagined that the duke's wealth, while great, would be sparingly directed at himself. Other than his indulgences for sartorial finery and superior provends, his wants were few. His palace, while impressive for its harmonious architecture and lovely gardens, was of a humble plan. The furnishings were simple: sturdy chairs, settees, plain carpets. The artwork spare, save for a portrait or two. And the bedroom wing was surprisingly small. It was necessary to put two sisters to a room. (This arrangement did much to inflame quarreling, as the sisters were accustomed to their privacy.) Whether this was the result of living alone—he had never married—or a preference for simplicity, the abbess could not tell. But she was approving of his charity, kindness, and devotion to God. And the sisterhood, upon settling in, delighted in his generosity.

In honor of their monastic ways, he had removed himself from the palace and set up house in one of the outer buildings on the estate.

And it was at this palace, in the shadows of the Duke of Ronda's estate, that Adela's romance with the playwright had developed, with all the exhilaration of physical delight. Their favorite meeting place: the secret garden. How lovely and verdant, in the very center of a maze that tricked all who tried to find it. Only the gardener, old Pablo, knew the shortest, most direct way to its center.

Never could Adela have imagined how deliriously happy she might feel to experience the mystery of a man.

And yet, as the weeks passed, Hernán, despite his amorous displays and sweet words, was unable to pledge his troth. Alone in her room she closed her eyes and remembered every detail of their first tryst on the palace grounds. That night the winds had been so strong they relieved the almond trees of all their petals. And there, on the palace's ground, was a coverlet of blossoms so sweet in scent, so soft of touch that Hernán and Adela had gone barefoot on the lawns to find the maze's hidden alcove. It was like walking on the finest of silk. White as the snow of the Sierra Nevada. Hand in hand, they stepped into the boxwood puzzle, a flush of greenery, snaking and curling, sometimes tightly and, then, suddenly wide. There were forks and bends beckoning them to go this way and that.

"Look," Hernán had whispered, "let us go here," as Adela pulled his hand in the opposite direction.

"All right, love," she would answer again and again, allowing him to lead.

Yes, that was the night of many truths revealed. Truths about his intentions and hers. Finally, they entered the alcove garden at the maze's core. And it was beautiful indeed. Six orange trees in flower were planted round its rim. The grass was short and sweet. And then it happened. Everything around them, plant and bird and sky and wind had simply disappeared. Only his skin and her skin, breath, tears, sighs made up the world.

"My love?" she had asked when at last they were sated, "is this forever? Or a fancy? Am I yours; are you mine?"

Silence.

He had answered with a sigh,

And silence again.

"Let us just enjoy the moment, my heart," he had answered, finally. "For however long we have. You must remember I am bound by Court. The King. I have duties."

She could feel her throat constrict, and then his hands upon her cheeks as she swallowed in shame.

46

carefully

After the nuns had spent their first week at the palace, the bishop paid a visit to the sisterhood, with the express purpose of having a certain conversation with Mother Ana. These days, he was furious at the abbess. He blamed her for his sister's total breakdown. How he had come to dread his daily life, with Soledad Paz, now an invalid.

He had already inspected the monastery, entering each room on all three floors to determine the extent of decay. He had thought, prior to this inspection, to secure funds—perhaps asking his counterparts in Castilla—to repair the destruction. This had been his intention.

But upon entering the premises of the venerable building, whatever illusions he might have had of restoring the lovely old convent vanished. So great was the ruin on the first floor that he came to believe that never would the Church be able to justify the expense. And anyway their order was in dire straits. Who knew if they were heading for the rack?

He was startled by the growth of mold that seemed to drape each wall, indeed every surface, of what had once been a luxurious residence. The paintings were covered in black slime. The curtains, too.

The odor was insufferable and noxious. And pests were feeding upon this filth in every room.

Yes, he supposed, there was some justification in trying to restore the convent; it had a long and remarkable history. But, wouldn't it be easier to transfer the community to another monastery? Surely, the sisterhood of Agnes could accommodate them.

As he waited in the library to talk privately with the abbess, these thoughts informed his determination to speak authoritatively, so as to prevent any dialogue with the willful woman. For he knew that she would object vociferously. She might even overpower his argument with her trickery. This he must avoid at all cost.

He would take the lead. He would command.

Stroking his ruby ring, he closed his eyes. Yes.

"Dear Bishop," he heard in just that moment. And there, stepping through the door, was the Reverend Mother, walking with a considerable limp. "How nice of you to come. How thoughtful of you."

Abbess Ana was, if not shrewd, then the most determined of women. Nothing on earth, no temporal power or authority, could keep her from her mission and her goals. And so before she had received word from the bishop of his impending visit, she had prepared herself for the official Church reaction to Saint Margaret's misfortune. (And she also knew the weaknesses of the bishop, having carefully observed him from her special vantage point throughout the years. She knew that he was beset by two, quite major, vices: thinking himself superior, as man, to nuns, no matter how capable and self-sufficient the latter might be, and putting the wants and whims of the bishopric's coffers—and his stomach—above all else.)

In his arrogance, he had overlooked certain details about Saint Margaret's that might have proven educational, if not revelatory, thinking that what he saw on the convent's surface was its reality. He had assumed, for instance, that the wealth displayed in its halls and rooms was the outcome of good business, more specifically, the successful commissioning of lace.

Because the bishop thought he knew the source of the convent's wealth, he never looked as carefully as he might have at the particulars of its luxury. For it was in these particulars, the minute details of its decoration and refurbishment, that the true story of the convent could be found.

And, so, the bishop's certain conversation with the abbess took a path he could never have expected.

"And how good of you to receive me in your sadness, dear Abbess," replied the bishop as the abbess, with considerable effort, sat down on the settee in the grand hall of the Duke of Ronda's palace.

The bishop, with all the authority that the Church had given him, then made his case before the abbess: that most, most, unfortunately Saint Margaret could not be rescued, as the cost was far too dear.

"Oh, but indeed there is no problem whatsoever, dear Bishop," she replied. "The cost shall be carried by Don Ramón, my brother, or shall I say my brother's estate, a most wealthy estate in New Castile. His entire wealth is mine to share, you see. And I shall take it upon myself, dear Bishop, to rebuild Saint Margaret's. And let me say, emphatically, that we will begin at once. And the Duke of Ronda, bless his soul, has kindly agreed to let us stay here until the abbey is restored."

The bishop smiled weakly. For once again the abbess Ana proved to be a worthy navigator of ecclesiastical politics.

"We hope, rather, it is our sincere wish, to present the Easter pageant next week, a little later than planned, before the King. Señor de Vigo has arranged this with the duke. We will present the work in the ballroom. We hope we have the honor of your presence, dear Bishop."

The prelate nodded. "One thing more, my dear Abbess Ana," the bishop said, as he stood up before her.

"Yes, Reverend Bishop," returned the abbess as she stood up, too.

"There have been reports against the sisterhood. Reports of, shall I say, impropriety. And the Holy Office has taken note of such. And, I think you should be well aware that the sister Adela has been identified as a heretic. Even worse. Much worse, I am afraid."

"And what is that, dare I ask?"

"Reports have been prepared. Adela must be taken from the convent. There will be a trial, I am told. Credible evidence exists against her. Did you not know, dear Abbess, that she consorts with magic? My sister has seen this with her very own eyes! And Isabela is her accomplice. She is suspect too. In fact, the entire convent is now under watch because of these two miscreants."

"Ah, well, dear Bishop, I do not know how this can be. As we, all of us, and especially Adela, endeavor in all of our labors and in our prayers to serve God in every way we can. And Adela and Isabela are most faithful. Most faithful indeed." The abbess could feel her chest tighten.

The bishop bowed, ever so slightly.

"But we are ready, dear Bishop, for whatever investigation you think worthy of such reports, as you say, against us. In fact, I should welcome them. Yes. I should. For Our Lord is with us. This I know."

The abbess made the sign of the cross upon her heart.

"And, now Your Grace, I must go to my daughters. To pray."

Yes, thought the abbess, it is time to tell my daughters of the bishop. Of his arrogance and pride. For years she had wondered about the nature of the prelate, but now she knew that her suspicion was the outcome of her accurate estimation.

Who was the bishop? On the surface, she supposed, he was no better, no worse than any other prelate in the kingdom. He luxuriated in the meditative spirit of his serene palace; he endeavored to practice the faith, albeit with fanfare and some pomposity; he presided over the abbey and other monasteries with wavering attention; offered communion to his flock; upheld the sacraments, managed vast properties with maniacal precision. Yes, he was no better, no worse. Except for one inconvenient fact: he had betrayed his flock, the sisters of Saint Margaret's.

It was time to act. And quickly. To protect her dearest. To protect them all. But what to do?

Three
1580

47

relativity

The abbess sat still, ever so still, in her chair, holding a small glass of *aguardiente*. She was reflecting on the events of the past nine months on this her saint day, January 28. The Virgin's account of what would befall the sisterhood had been so truthful, so decidedly correct, that the abbess marveled at the Holy Virgin's prophecy. Yes, the Mother of God had been taken by a flood from her blessed home at Saint Margaret. Yes, the convent had been reduced to a ruin. And, yes, by the grace of *El Señor*, Saint Margaret's had been rebuilt.

Not so far from the convent, in a labyrinthine quarter of the ancient city—the old Jewish quarter—there lived a master foreman, Delbourgo, or "*el genio*" as he was known. One morn with the help of the Duke of Ronda she had gone to visit him. The quarter, a neighborhood of merchants, had been a favorite destination of the abbess since she was made prioress. And it was to the spice market that she made yearly visits, not only because she liked cumin, coriander, and pepper on her food but because the spices themselves, heaped in baskets, flowing upon each other's rich tapestries, were beautiful to behold. Sensual reminders of the fertility of earth.

Putting her hands to her brow, she had peered intently at a heaping basket of saffron. Then, altering her focus, she looked at the tanned merchant across the way.

"Sister," called out the man, "who do you seek?"

"I seek the builder Delbourgo," she replied.

"It is I."

The abbess then noticed that he was carrying a bag of tools.

"What would you have me do, dear Sister?"

"Repair my chapel."

He had heard, as had much of the citizenry of Granada, that the convent's first floor had been nearly destroyed by a flood and that only recently had it been reopened after extensive cleaning. And he had also heard from the baker Molina that it was the abbess herself who undertook this endeavor, paying for it with her own largesse.

And so that day the craftsman followed the abbess to Saint Margaret and began his labor, which had taken nearly a year to complete.

But rebuilt and remade did not equate to being the same as before. In its reconstitution, the Convent of Saint Margaret had been forever changed. It was a truly different place. Many precious things had been destroyed: treasured books, important letters, a particular picture of a saint, a rosary of old. A lovely chest, beautiful chairs. Heirloom carpets, a wall-hanging handed down from a beloved grandmother. Such accoutrements had been plentiful. And among the convent's most precious possession, the greatest loss of all was dear Mary. At this thought, the abbess squinted her eyes to hold back tears. Whatever would have become of the sisters if the Duke of Ronda had not been so hospitable? Relegated to the poor Convent of Saint Agnes, as the bishop had so blithely suggested? And how would they have managed. Twice the number of its occupants in such a cramped, impoverished place? And a distressing doubling, indeed, for Saint Margaret's sisterhood was beyond frazzled. And Dulzura had become a veritable curse. What a torture to them all.

The abbess sipped her drink. Sighing, she thought: *But this is a feast day. Let me think of more joyful things instead.*

Our Dearest Lady, Mary. A very vision of the kindest human heart. She closed her eyes and remembered past feast days, when the Holy Mother had been with them. How very early in the morn the abbess would go to the chapel to offer Mary treasures of the larder.

The best and most delectable confections: sherbets of fruits and almond cakes. Raisins and prunes. Duck paté and sausage. How grateful the Holy Mother was to receive such treats.

As the abbess clasped her rosary, she remembered, too, the time when Mary told her of her wedding day. She had worn a shift of rose linen and sandals of hemp. Her hair had been twisted at the nape, held in place by a flaxen thread and pin. She had been so frightened, but Joseph had held her hand throughout the day, as if it were a newborn dove, so tenderly. Dear Joseph. *What an honorable man*, thought the abbess, as she sipped yet again.

Ah, Mary, thought the abbess. I miss you, Heavenly Mother.

The abbess closed her eyes and prayed.

> Dear Lord,
>
> Forgive me all my sins, those that I have committed and those I have omitted. For any wrong that I have put upon another. For any hurt or affliction. I am your humble servant, Ana. May I do good on your behalf. May I lead the sisterhood in meditative excellence. May I help to heal their sadness, sorrows, pains, both of heart and body. Dear Lord, I beseech thee to uphold my resolve, to renew my efforts to follow your example. Amen.

As the last bell of the night rang forth, Adela walked to the chapel. Tears fell down her cheeks as she thought of different times, not so long ago, when Hernán was with them. What had she lost or gained in loving so? She might never know. Sometimes she felt a fool. But, then again, she felt blessed for having been kissed and held and told that she was beautiful. She had loved. She had felt the intensity of passion. How could this be bad?

She entered the dimly lit sanctuary. There it was: the pink marble altar. Now, carefully, she placed upon it the offering of her heart, the offering of Milagros's love, the offering of the Alhambra caterpillars. Her sorrow and her joy. She had sewn together the pieces left to her by fate, the flood, and God. What had remained. This was her altar cloth. A cloth of three subjects, three faiths.

She looked at the lovely lace, which shimmered with gold threads, and saw that it was curling round the edge. What to do? For this cloth for the holy altar must be perfect.

Taking her little basket of needles, thread, and keepsakes, she sorted out the glassy baubles. Twenty in all. Like stones in weight. Then, guessing at their effect, she placed each one inside the little pockets.

The hem was even. Perfect. Straight.

Meanwhile, on that night of collective ruminations, memories, and commemoration, Victoria wept. No longer could she see. The last little spark of vision was gone. As Victoria clasped her hands in prayer, she asked the Holy Mother for peace.

And a miracle had taken place that night, too. For Sister Dulzura. Why it had occurred none of the sisters, including the anointed nun herself, would ever know. But it happened all the same. Dulzura, feeling ill from something that she had eaten at supper—most certainly a pork empanada gone bad—was thinking about revenge. She would show that dim-witted cook, Isabela, what she deserved.

She had turned on her side, to relieve the pressure in her belly when, suddenly, there was Mary before her. Not the statue of their beloved Holy Mother, but Mary, the very Queen in radiant beauty in her resplendent gown of azure, holding up her hand.

"Dulzura, do you see this onion?" asked the Virgin.

"Yes, Holy Mother."

"You must eat it," and the Virgin handed it to her. "Eat it now. All of it."

As Dulzura obeyed the Virgin, she began to cry great tears, for the onion's juices were so sharp, so fiery that she could barely force herself to swallow them.

"These are the bitter juices that you have applied to Saint Margaret's consecration, the body of her spirit."

As Dulzura struggled to finish the onion, blubbering and feeling sorry for herself, the Virgin continued. "You have a choice, tonight, my daughter. To forever change your ways. To choose right or to choose wrong."

And the Virgin held up to the moonlight, coming through Dulzura's window, a star of marzipan.

It was thus that sister Dulzura was forever healed of her hateful self. She made a promise to the Holy Mother: no longer would she torment her sisters with gibes, needles, worms, vilifications, beetles, derisions, red ants, or taunts.

And then, before the Virgin Mother left Saint Margaret, she visited the cell of little Beatriz.

"You are chosen among my daughters," said the Virgin as the little girl looked up to see the Heavenly Mother floating before her. "You will grow in grace and you will perform miracles of healing. You are favored by my Son. One day you shall lead this nunnery, as Abbess Ana has done so well."

And then the Virgin simply disappeared.

Before she fell asleep, the abbess received a revelation from her Lord and God. "Ana," she heard, as if the voice were hidden underneath the sound of human voice, a tone of clarity, understandable and powerful yet of an ineffable composition. "You, who are named after my own dearest grandmother Saint Anne, must rededicate the abbey to good works."

The abbess, crossing herself, could not help but feel a bright and glorious joy.

"But how dear Lord?" she answered softly.

"By faith and acts of faith. Faith that it can be so. And acts of faith that will strengthen thee and yours."

And that is how she came to understand that Saint Margaret should no longer be dedicated to the making of lace. The time had come for other pursuits. Yes. Her flock would make new sacrifices. They would henceforth dedicate themselves not to the making of fineries but to good works and works of faith, as servants of the Lord. The lace room would become a place of schooling for girls. They would expand the office of their infirmary so as to attend to indigent women with child; they would establish a kitchen to feed the poor.

48

finality

Since returning to Madrid at the behest of His Majesty the King, Hernán had enjoyed a most accommodating life, both personally and professionally. Delighting in the playwright's sacred one-acts and sonnets, the Sovereign often asked him for small entertainments in the late evenings, after the royal court had dined. And the bevy of lovely women in the palace, ladies-in-waiting all, provided Hernán with his own entertainment in turn. One such beauty, a certain Carmen Josefina, had become his nightly diversion. So energetically artful was she in the sack that he could no longer count on a good night's sleep. Why did a man have to choose one woman over another when the world was full of such exquisite creatures? Surely, he deserved as many feminine delights as he might find along the course of his days.

And yet, for certain, he did think often of the sweet Adela, the fair and guileless maiden. She was very pretty, too. But certainly not the prettiest lover he had known. It was her soul, he supposed, that kept him bound to her in some way. A depth of goodness that he had never found in any other woman. She was trusting. Too trusting, poor creature. But what could he do? He was not made for marriage, of this he was certain. And they did enjoy a passion, however brief. With time she would come to understand.

And what to do about his report? The Holy Office had sent two emissaries demanding the completed dossier of his investigations. If indeed they were to try this wicked Adela and her accomplice, Isabela, the sooner the better. Time was of the essence. The bishop had provided overwhelming evidence against them. All that was needed now was the investigator's report.

Hernán's outrage at the nagging persistence of these ecclesiastical overlords and the vigor of their intent to harm the young woman (one of his women!) and involve the naïve Isabela, too, had led him to at least one decision. He must, at all costs, find a way to protect them. And so that evening, forgoing his romp with the talented Josefina, he sat down and composed the dreaded but necessary missive. It read as follows:

> Your Excellencies,
>
> I would have written sooner but the demands of the Court have been my first priority. The King has commissioned me to write two morality plays for his saint day. And I am working on a comedia as well. Forgive me the delay, as I know how eagerly you await my report regarding la Señora Soledad Paz's denouncement of the sisterhood of Saint Margaret.
>
> As you know I took this assignment most seriously. And I endeavored to act with utmost discretion in my investigations. For this reason, alone, did I engage the sisterhood in acts of theatre, so as to understand their motivations and spirits. I was the director. They were my actors. The stage was my making.
>
> I studied them, as they studied their parts. And they did take them up with great enthusiasm, getting lost in the spirit of rhetoric and mimesis.
>
> Thus, was I able to watch them off-guard, so to speak.
>
> In addition, I took pains to observe them in their labor and their meditative practice. During the day and during the night.
>
> Your Graces, the accusations made against Saint Margaret were grave, indeed. And seriously did I take my assignment.
>
> I now list for you the only incidents I ever found to raise the slightest hint of laxity, whether ecclesiastical or moral.

Number one. I did see that the child Beatriz can levitate. But, Your Lords, I have heard on the highest authority that the Sister Teresa of Avila is also beset by such levitations. And are you not, Your Lords, impressed—if begrudgingly—by that remarkable nun? So, perhaps, you will agree that the little Beatriz, rather than show any deviancy from the faith, is actually rather blessed. A chosen one, shall we say? For that, Your Graces, is what I do believe. She has been anointed by Our Lord.

Number two. There is a sister among them who is truly a thorn to the community. A peculiar woman. Disagreeable in the extreme. And of mean feature and form. She appears to be a kind of carbuncle on the face of things at Saint Margaret. She is kept at a distance by all, as her spirit is so dark as to poison human interaction. While her spirit and her actions are of a low grade, I feel that we must pity her. For, did not Saint Paul have a conversion, himself being of the lowest order of mankind and finding his way to the true religion on the road to Damascus? I believe that this nun too can be redeemed. Perhaps we should pray for this poor soul, as Christ taught us to do.

Number three. According to Soledad Paz, the sister of Granada's bishop, the nuns take baths more than twice a year. Yes, this is true. The baths at Saint Margaret are beautiful and central to the compound. Sisters take baths nearly every day. But there is, I believe, a simple and compelling reason for this, Your Graces. The sisterhood at Saint Margaret makes the most exquisite lace in the land. You will agree. And it is of great importance that the lace produced be of perfection, unstained, unsoiled. The heat of Granada, as you well know, can cause copious oils of the body. The sisterhood, it was explained to me by Abbess Ana, must be clean each day so as to not stain their handiwork, with either soil from the earth—they are obe-dient gardeners—or sweat from their brow or hands. It is with reverence that they spin their lace, lace that is to be worn by the royal household and aristocracy of the land (not to mention Your Excellencies). They wish their lace to be as pure as the hearts of those who wear it. It is thus that they cleanse their bodies as often as they cleanse their souls.

Number four. As for gluttonous tendencies. Having lived among the sisterhood and eaten of their table, I can attest to the magnificent quality of their provends. So gifted are the sisters at cookery, that their dishes made me swoon. Particularly, a cake with pomegranate sauce and pudding of cream and rice. Excellencies, is it the sisters' fault that they have such a noble kitchen in their midst? If any of them are to blame for enjoyment of delicacies, then I, too, am guilty. For I succumbed to the pleasure of such foodstuffs, again and again. (The chocolate is extraordinary.)

Number five. As for the claims that the sister Adela consorts with magic, that she recites incantations and talks to the Devil— perhaps the gravest of all accusations made by la Señora Paz—I cannot say. I did not witness such behavior. Ever. With all due respect to the accuser, it was simply not evident to me. And as for the matter of her hermitage. Once I did enter it to find nothing save a scrap of cloth. A bit of her handiwork. If anything, I believe this nun to be obedient to Our Lord . . . in the extreme. She is modest, humble, caring in all her ways. The same can be said for the young Isabela. I realize you might disagree with my findings, but I can do no other than to speak the truth as I know it.

With reverence, and in keeping with the One and Only Faith,

Hernán de Vigo Gómez

After he had finished this epistle, he took a bottle of brandy from the cupboard, poured himself a generous amount, and gulped down his glass. Then, he lay down on his bed and fell asleep.

49

faintly

One evening, shortly after the abbess had announced her new plans for the sisterhood, a messenger from the Duke of Ronda arrived at the convent. Knocking at the gate, he was soon met by Isabela.

"I will wait here," he said, after handing her a parcel for the abbess. Rushing to the Reverend Mother's rooms, Isabela gave the message to her superior. The abbess unraveled the roll of parchment to find another epistle within, waxed with a large, red seal. It read:

> Esteemed Reverend Mother,
>
> It is arranged. Be confident. The postulants, Adela and Isabela, must leave the convent at once. A source dear to me has ascertained the girls' imminent arrest. Tomorrow, I am told, a cavalcade is being sent to the convent to get them. My envoy will bring the maidens to my palace this evening. I will take them under cover of night to Cadiz. There they will be met by my cousin who has arranged for their passage to New Castile. The girls will be safely delivered to your brother, Don Ramón; rest assured, dear Abbess. And as for the inquiries of the King,

should he persist in asking for their presence at El Escorial, you need not worry. I will find a way to placate my uncle. He has always enjoyed a good tale with a surprise ending better than a tiresome dictation of verisimilitude.

Ronda

The abbess instructed Isabela to fetch Adela. "Gather your things, my dear. And tell Adela to do the same. Then, come back quickly."

Soon, the three women were alone in the abbess's rooms.

Gesturing that they should kneel, the Reverend Mother placed a hand on each. "There are matters of which I haven't told you, my dears; things that concern your safety. I have thought it best to spare you, for the forces that would harm you are contradictory to the true teachings of Our Lord, and they would be as detrimental to your kind dispositions as they would to your sweet souls. But you must understand that danger is at hand. The Duke of Ronda awaits you. He will protect you. Soon you will be far away, in a happier clime. Now rise."

Then taking each daughter in her arms, first Adela and then Isabela, she softly spoke again.

"Remember, the Lord is with you, always. And Mother Mary resides in your heart. Commit yourselves to love. Seek joy and purpose. All will be well, dear Daughters. All will be well."

four
1581

50

generosity

Standing at the window, she saw wide, somnolent clouds. The salt air mist. In this new place, where seagulls swooped and sighed, she knew a very different beauty from that in Granada. This was a euphoric town full of clanging bells and wildness.

Below her, in the plaza, blue-eyed doves perched wherever there was generosity. Musicians played fanciful tunes. Mules, carrying ecclesiastical treasures, paraded over cobblestone. Swaggering soldiers danced with *doncellas*. In one corner of the square, naked children played and, opposite, a group of old women whistled, while selling their goods.

She had been in Lima, Ciudad de los Reyes one year, and, still, each morning the scene outside her window seemed as fresh and interesting as the first day she saw it.

Sailing across the sea, often frightened and ill, she had worried about their fate. What would become of her and Isabela?

Day after day on that monotonous voyage, though they had prayed for strength of spirit, they had found more comfort in telling make believe. Stories upheld them.

But neither could have imagined the story they inhabited now. She was content, even happy here, yes.

Oh, such magnificence—the sky, redolent with its own tracery of lace and the other fineries of God—was hers to cherish each day, as was love.

"Sister Adela," she heard Isabela playfully say behind her, before lifting her eyes. "Your husband awaits you. Don Ramón says come."

Harmony is created of opposites.

Lope de Vega

Author's Note

A Stitch in Air was born of two experiences decades apart. The first was a two-day visit to a convent in Southern Spain when I was a junior in college studying in Madrid. Easter Week I decided to leave the capital to travel to Andalucía to see the great cities of Sevilla, Córdoba, and Granada. Along the way, I stopped to meet the aunt of one of my professors back home in the States. He told me that she would welcome me and that I would find my encounter with her very interesting. What an understatement! She, along with the other nuns in her monastery in Murcia, left a lasting impression on me . . . for their warm humor, witty conversation, and hospitality. The second experience occurred on a trip to Brussels, Belgium in 2008. Among the many museums I visited there was the Musée du Costume et de la Dentelle, which is a repository of extraordinary European lace made throughout the ages. There was one example that truly captivated me: a circumcision cloth dating back to the sixteenth century. As I stared at the exquisite craftsmanship of the fabric, I had an epiphanic moment: I would write a novel about a group of Spanish sisters, lace makers, in the fifteen hundreds.

A Stitch in Air owes much of its detail to visits I have made to monasteries in Avila in addition to the books I have read about old convents, lacemaking, the Spanish Inquisition, the city of Granada, and the wonders of Al-Andalus. The books that were the most influential to my imaginings that I consulted are: *The Romance of Lace* by Mary Eirwen Jones; *Daily Life During the Spanish Inquisition* by James M. Anderson; *The Arts of Intimacy: Christians, Jews, and Muslims in the Making of Castilian Culture* by Jerrilynn D. Dodds, María Rosa Menocal, and Abigail Krasner Balbale; *Women and Miracle Stories*, edited by Anne-Marie Korte; *Ordering Women's Lives* by Julie Ann Smith; *The Three Rings: The History of the Spanish Jews* by Poul Borchsenius; and *Nuns Behaving Badly* by Craig A. Monson. My sources of quotations and attributions in the novel are as follows: on page 11 is a saying of Saint Anthony of Padua, which I found in Diane Watt, ed., *Medieval Women in Their Communities* (Toronto: University of Toronto Press, 1997), 72; on pages 16 and 17 is the *Teresa de Avila prayer*; on page 75 is a poem by Elizabeth Mackett, a seventeenth-century English lace maker, which was taken from Annie Louise Potter, *A Living Mystery* (A. J. Publishing International, 1990).

While some readers might be surprised at the occasionally irreverent tone of my book, I'd like to note that certain women who lived in convents during the time in which this novel takes place were less than thrilled about it. These women felt isolated, lonely, frustrated, and desirous of affection and sex. A few succumbed to despair. And women who didn't necessarily have a religious vocation sometimes lived out their days in convents, too. I wrote my story with those countless, nameless souls in mind. I just listened and put their tales down on the page as best I could, and I exercised novelistic license when needed. Perhaps a reader or two will see a resemblance between Hernán de Vigo and that "monster of nature" Lope de Vega.

In addition to the aforementioned texts that helped me during the creation of my story is an institution that offered me support of various kinds: The American Academy in Rome. To the entire staff of this incomparable treasure on the Janiculum Hill, I say, "Grazie, grazie." And thanks from my heart as well to my husband Oscar Hijuelos, my family, my agent Jennifer Lyons, Judy Sternlight, my editor Irene Vilar, Christina Askounis, Susan Bennitt, Karen Levinson, and the team at Texas Tech University Press.

Lori Marie Carlson

About the Author

Lori Marie Carlson is an editor, translator, and novelist whose numerous books include the landmark anthology, *Cool Salsa,* and the novels, *The Sunday Tertulia* and *The Flamboyant.* She divides her time between New York City and Durham, North Carolina, where she teaches in the English Department at Duke University.